I HAVE THE SIGHT

EDWARD KING BOOK ONE

RICK WOOD

BLOOD SPLATTER PRESS

ABOUT THE AUTHOR

Rick Wood is a British writer born in Cheltenham.

His love for writing came at an early age, as did his battle with mental health. After defeating his demons, he grew up and became a stand-up comedian, then a drama and English teacher, before giving it all up to become a full-time author.

He now lives in Loughborough, where he divides his time between watching horror, reading horror, and writing horror.

Rick also publishes thrillers under the pseudonym Ed Grace...

Jay Sullivan

Assassin Down

Kill Them Quickly

The Bars That Hold Me

A Deadly Weapon

For the ghosts of my mind that proved that demons can be defeated.

MILLENNIUM NIGHT

CHAPTER ONE

*E*ddie places a wary step onto the porch, feeling it sink. He takes his hands from his pockets. Tucks in his shirt. Tries to flatten hair that just springs back up again.

One needs to be presentable, Derek had lectured him. *Whether you are meeting the mother or taking on the very depths of hell, a pulled-up tie and a welcoming smile are essential parts of an exorcist's uniform.*

The porch itself is a mess of weeds entangling cracked wooden beams, loosely holding up the porch roof. The light above his head flickers. The wooden tiles moan under his feet.

The house itself looks just as erratic and flimsy as this porch.

But Eddie has no choice.

In this house is a girl in dire need of intervention.

A girl named Adeline, who stands no chance without him.

And inside Adeline is something Eddie is eager to meet.

He attempts the doorbell and waits. There is no sound of ringing in the house and, after waiting a few minutes, he knocks on the door instead. Four assertive knocks, equally paced, to announce his arrival. Knocking in fours comforts him, puts him at ease; makes him feel calm, as even numbers always have.

A sound of shuffling grows louder. He stands patiently as the numerous locks and bolts are unshackled, one by one. Once every barrier from the outside is opened, the door creaks ajar, revealing half a woman's face. There are bags beneath her eye, her eyebrows are bushy and unkempt, and the wrinkles of her forehead appear defined.

"Good morning," he greets her, quelling his impatience and forcing a smile. "I'm here for Adeline."

"Are you... *him?*" whispers the woman.

There is a mixture of wariness and optimism in her voice. It is the same voice he has heard numerous times before — it is the voice of a mother at the end of her tether, clinging on to him as her very last hope.

"Yes, ma'am, I am," he assures her. "May I come in?"

The woman nods with a surge of renewed energy and stares at her saviour. Eventually, she realises she actually needs to open the door, and she tugs the splintered wooden slab inwards, allowing him to step over the threshold.

It is chilly outside, but in here is even colder.

She leads him into a kitchen. The room is a dreadful mess, full of dirty pots, pans, and mouldy remains of meals scattered over the surfaces. Blacked-out windows make him realise why the woman was squinting at the light behind him as he stood in the doorway. He peers into the corridor and notices that the blackened windows are a consistent feature throughout the house.

He takes her hand in his and holds it.

She flinches at first, wary of what he is doing, but his soothing smile calms her, and she lets him take her cold, clammy hand in his and shake it, as one would in a customary greeting.

"How have you been?" is the first thing he asks her.

"Not… Not so good." Her voice is shaking, and she is clearly fighting the urge to well up.

"I can imagine. The windows — did you do this?"

"Yes. Yes, I, er… the light. It hurt her. She burned when she was near it."

"Did she?"

He places his bag on the ground and removes his coat.

"Er, may I?" he asks, spotting an unused coat hook on the door. She shrugs her shoulders and stutters over a few inaudible sounds. He takes that as a yes and hangs his coat.

He steps into the hallway and pauses by the stairs. She follows behind, scuttling like a beetle, led like a rat to the Pied Piper.

He glances at pictures fastened to the walls. There's one of a family on the beach — a mother, father and daughter, smiling, arms around each other.

"Is this her?"

"Yes… that was her. Before…" The woman looks away. Her arms quiver. He can see her breath in the air.

He studies the picture for a few moments. The girl in this picture is smiling. She has braces, but they do not detract from how pretty she is.

He looks at the next picture along. It is of the girl in a play, centre stage, her mouth opened wide. He imagines a beautiful singing voice coming out of it.

"Does she like performing?"

"Yes… she did…"

He nods. He turns his attention to the woman before him.

"So, Miss Copple. Beatrice. Is it okay if I call you Beatrice?"

She shrugs her shoulders.

"Call me whatever you like," she answers. "Just please save my daughter."

He leans toward her, placing hands upon her shoulders.

"I assure you, Beatrice. There is nothing that will defeat me."

Her hands clasp together as if in jubilant prayer, and her face becomes overjoyed, forcing a smile through the tears and pain.

"Can I meet Adeline?" he asks, peering upstairs.

"You can. But I assure you... What is up there is not Adeline."

"I understand. Would it be okay if I were to meet — *it* — alone?"

Beatrice nods weakly.

He takes the first step, then the next, and the next. The cold deepens as he ascends, the steps creaking harder, and something comes at him, like a surge of evil, getting stronger, bigger, grander.

He pauses at the top. Looks at the bedroom to his left. The mother's room, with an unmade bed surrounded by tissues. Before him is a bathroom with a protruding odour he tries to ignore.

And to his right, a closed bedroom door.

He hears breathing — deep, sinister breathing. He can feel the hatred, the anger, the terror, all exuding from the exposed crevices that expose no light.

He enters the room.

Inside, it's even colder. Ripped paper lies strewn across the floor, and the table and chairs are broken into pieces. The wallpaper is ripped and the paint cracked. The walls are covered in some form of Latin writing and demonic drawings.

On the single bed before him, laying upon ripped white sheets stained in red, is a girl.

The girl's hands and feet are individually buckled to the corners of the bed. The wrists, heavily restrained, are scratched and bleeding. She wears a nighty, but barely; it is ripped and torn, revealing her pale and bruised naked flesh. She lays on the bed with her belly and crotch sticking up in the air.

This is not Adeline.

In body, yes — but her mind and her soul are elsewhere.

It turns its head and directs its evil eyes toward him. The pupils are fully dilated, her face marked with open wounds, and her lips cracked and peeled. It laughs. But not the kind of laugh you would expect from a teenage girl; it is a deep, crackling laughter that explodes through him, reverberating against his bones and sending a freezing chill down his spine.

"Hello, Adeline. Hello, evil spirit that dwells inside. Do you have a name, or should I just continue with 'evil spirit'?"

The laughter grows louder. It is no longer laughter aimed at disturbing him; it is laughter of genuine humour, mocking the confidence he has brought into the room.

"Laugh all you want, demon. I have faced your brothers, and your sisters, and they were all far worse than you."

"My brothers?" it speaks slowly, deeply, pronouncing each syllable with venom, as if every word is intended to mock him. "What do you know of my brothers?"

"I know of one I fought in Bath last week that had taken hold of a nine-year-old girl. It squealed like a pig when I got it out of her." He takes a step forward, snarling at the creature that does not appear the slightest bit intimidated. "I know of one in Devon a few months ago. I removed it from a woman and I cursed it until it cried. Tell me, demon…"

He stands directly over the bed, leaning slightly toward a face full of pure evil.

"What kind of sound will you make when I remove you from this child?"

The creature laughs again. "So you're the one who's come to save Adeline?"

"Yes, sir," he speaks clearly. "Yes I am."

1984

CHAPTER TWO

*S*he was always there. She was there when he slept, she was there when he woke up, and she was there when he died. There was no escape, and his fear only encouraged her.

He was eleven the first time he saw her. He was riding his bike, chasing his sister through the curving roads of his estate, laughing merrily.

"I'll catch you!" he teased, eager to play a game with her. Eager to make her like him. But they were going too fast. They were skidding onto the opposite side of the road as they turned the corners, such was their speed.

"Slow down!" he cried out, but the wind nulled his words before they reached her.

"Cassy, stop!" he bellowed.

She turned her head, trying to hear what he was saying, meaning she did not see the car pulling out of the driveway.

Blood adorned the pavement as her body spun and twisted over the bonnet. Her limp body landing on the road was the last thing Eddie saw before he was hit.

* * *

EDDIE AWOKE in a state of confusion. He lifted his head. He was not in the estate anymore. He was not in the road. He was not next to the car.

He pushed himself to his knees, feeling his head for cuts and bruises.

Nothing.

He had pummelled into a car at full speed and nothing. No pain in his legs, no marks on his skin, no weakness in his bones. In fact, he wasn't breathing at all. His heart wasn't beating and his lungs weren't expanding, yet he felt as alive as ever.

He was in what felt like a box, yet he couldn't see the walls that contained him. His surroundings were white — bright-white, almost blindingly so. It was warm, but there was no sun.

He took one step forward and the illumination dropped.

The white collapsed, as if it was a cloth being pulled away. Behind it was a volcanic pit. Beneath him, the ground turned into rock, surrounded by spewing, boiling lava, churning and lashing at his bare feet.

He edged forward, gauging his surroundings, peering left, then right. The bump of the stones was hot, and he pushed himself to the tip of his toes to avoid scorching the base of his feet.

His lip quivered, his arms shook, and the pit of his stomach twisted. He could hear cackling reverberating around him, but could see nothing. Nothing was there. He was isolated. It felt as if all hope had disappeared from the world and there was nothing he could do.

The mound of stones fell from beneath, plummeting him into vacant chaos. He flailed his frantic arms, reaching out with stretched fingers to clutch onto something that might save him.

It was no good.

His scream was silenced by the lashing of flames. For a moment, the heat consumed him and he was in agony, feeling every cell in his body die. The flames latched onto his skin and lingered. He closed his eyes, trying to endure, feeling the heat burn through his skin, his bones, his muscle...

When he landed, the lava had gone, and he was surrounded by a grey fog that formed misty cloaks over faded grass. Dead trees hung like a mobile over a baby's cot, surrounding graves, nature at its most sinister. He displayed no scars, no marks, no remnants of the fiery pit.

As he lifted his head and his eyes fell on the words upon the gravestone before him, he recoiled in sickening horror.

CASSY KING
1976 – 1984
Gone and forgotten, never to be seen again.

HIS MOUTH FILLED with vomit and he spewed blood onto the hard ground. His hands instinctively clung onto the headstone, clawing at the words with fingers covered in dead skin.

He shook the headstone as if the words would disappear like an Etch A Sketch. He dragged his nails down it, hoping to scratch it off, ignoring the trails of blood left by his hands, praying the eulogy would turn to dust.

It didn't. If anything, it seemed to get bigger.

Shuffle, shuffle. The scrape of feet across pavement like a spade upon cement crept up behind him. Hugging the tombstone against his body, he twisted his head, turning to ice, his arms pulsating and his stomach churning. A cold wind accompanied the scrape, a rotting stench of death.

He saw the girl.

11

Though *girl* was not the right word to describe her…

Her jaw snapped with hunger. She dragged herself forward. Her bare feet scraped the surface with every slow limp, leaving a trail of blood in her wake. Her long, black, greasy hair fell in front of her face. She wore a stale gown painted with red handprints. He could see part of her thigh beneath the gown; it was pale and scarred, covered in slashes.

He could outrun her. He could, he knew it. Yet, he remained stationary, rooted to the spot with feet like lead.

He was transfixed.

He didn't understand why he wasn't running; somehow, she wasn't letting him.

He scrunched his eyes shut as she loomed ever closer. He felt her shadow engulf his, each of her breaths another hiss, a growl released with each exhale.

Her hands gripped his face. He flinched away. They were damp, cold, like stale ice, sending a shudder down his vertebrae, incapacitating him, sucking each joyful memory out of him.

"No!" He strained his voice in attempt to scream, but could make no sound. His voice had abandoned him.

Everything good in the world left. Nothing but evil remained — helpless, destitute, powerful evil.

He fell onto his back, losing the use of his arms, ceasing his grasp on the tombstone. Still, he couldn't crawl away, couldn't get away from the grip she seemed to have on him.

All he could see was her, snarling, dripping.

Her, her and nothing but her.

She inhaled him, prompting uncontrollable convulsions, raising his chest in the air. All senses abandoned him. He was empty. He was alone.

Rope protruded from the ground, entwining his arms in its roots, vines gripping his ankles, binding him.

She cackled.

No – *it* cackled. Its form was beyond that of a witch; it was that of a morbid, demented creature – pure, effervescent malevolence.

Behind the bitch was a booming laugh, reverberating through Eddie's chest. Its deep cackle entered his body, firing into his non-beating heart and expanding it against his ribs. His head was hefty, his hair connected to black, spiralled roots spurting from the ground. He put all his force into lifting his head and straining his eyes to see what was appearing before him.

There was another creature here now; three-headed, and exuding more manic and demonic energy than the black-haired beast. In fact, that 'female' beast fell to its knees and bowed before this other creature, acting as slave to its master.

"My name is *Balam*," roared the head of a man, bearded and scarred with mussy, fiery-red hair, wedged between the head of a snorting bull and a ram beating its head against its own body.

"My name is Balam," it repeated, its body mounted upon a sharply fanged bear. "And I have been waiting for you."

Eddie's head was allowed to peer up a fraction more, and he saw what Balam had in its claws.

Cassy.

A face full of tears, a ripped dress full of blood. Her skin was bruised. She reached out for her older brother, her arms grasping at nothing.

"Eddie!" Her mouth opened to scream, but was muted by the rawness of her throat, an empty breath of air protruding from her tender lungs.

"No!" Eddie cried, his love for his sister filling the never-ending surroundings. "Cassy!"

He pulled on his restraints with everything he had. Lifted every muscle, forced every strenuous movement.

It wasn't enough.

He barely moved.

And, in an instant, it was all taken away from him, and he awoke with a shriek.

In a hospital bed.

Plugged into beeping machines.

A dozen doctors burst into the room, laying him down, encouraging him to relax. But he couldn't, the image of Cassy being tormented by that... *whatever it was...* burnt onto the forefront of his mind.

He would come to learn that this coma, that had felt like minutes, had lasted weeks. He would soon find out that his sister was dead. He would know that his chasing her on their bikes had killed her.

He would have to grow up knowing his sister could have been alive if it weren't for him.

But it would take him far longer to learn what happened to her soul.

1987

CHAPTER THREE

*E*ddie sighed at his fumbling hands, feigning sincerity. Another day, another lecture; it grew old, and he was tired of it. It was always his fault. It was never them. Never.

"And, you little rat, if I catch you thieving again, I will wallop you so hard you'll go right through that soddin' wall, y'hear me?"

He lifted his head up to his father, fractionally raising his eyebrows but keeping his face otherwise blank; he knew his lack of reaction would incense him. Why was his father even trying to tell him off? He hardly knew right or wrong himself.

"Please, just stop fighting," piped up Eddie's mother, cowardly positioning herself at the back of the room.

Eddie snorted. He couldn't help it. His mum was trying to make it seem like she had the confidence to stand up to his dad, but Eddie wasn't deaf, nor was he blind. He heard the fights as they pounded through the walls at 2.00a.m. whilst he buried his face into his pillow. He saw the marks on her face that she passed off as *nothing, just a little disagreement.* He saw the look in her eyes, the look that said she wished she loved him enough to stand up to the bastard she shared a bed with, but was simply too weak.

They weren't the only ones suffering from Cassy's death. They weren't the only ones who needed support.

"I just can't believe you were so stupid," continued the overbearing, prematurely bald phony towering over him. "To pocket a chocolate bar. A chocolate bar, of all things, you steal."

"It's not about the chocolate bar…" Eddie muttered. He hoped his dad hadn't heard him.

His mother started edging closer, taking hold of her husband's arm and attempting to pull him away. His face was getting redder and his voice was increasing in pace; in addition to this, he was invading more and more of Eddie's personal space, breathing his alcoholic breath all over his son, turning into his natural, intimidating self.

"Please, don't," she requested feebly.

"Get off me," he replied, raising his arm and forcing her off balance. As she hit the ground, her head hit the wall. She stayed down, rubbing it, her eyelids fluttering.

"Mum!" Eddie rose to help her, but was shoved back down by the bulky fist of his egotistical dad.

Dad. Never has a term been less deserved…

Eddie didn't stick around to see what would happen next. As much as he wished he could help his mother, there was no point; she wasn't going to do anything about it. As much as he would love to help, it just hurt to watch his mother cower in front of the man who had once been such a devoted father-of-two.

Three years ago, this man was loving. He held Eddie in his arms and Eddie felt secure. No one would harm him. Then, since Cassy died…

He dodged his dad's swipe, darted through the hallway, and out the front door. His bike leant against the garage. He leapt upon it and shifted into second gear, spinning the pedals as fast as his heavy legs could manage.

The wind pounded against Eddie's eyes as he built up speed. His hair was unwashed and unkempt, greased into a firm position, and it felt nice to have a gust blowing against him. It was liberating.

Drops of rain flickered in the air and patted his face. He stopped pedalling, allowing the downhill tilt to carry him toward a house where he knew he was welcome, enjoying the damp security rain had always given him.

He arrived, dropped his bike into the hedge, grabbed the gutter, and shimmied his way up the brick wall of a warm, suburban family home. It was something he had done many times before. All it took was one knock on the window and it opened, allowing Eddie to climb in.

His best friend, Jenny, beheld him, her face full of concern. It was more than he could take. He gave in. Finally. The tears fell, drenching his cheeks and dampening his collar.

"It's okay," Jenny assured him, guiding him to the bed. She allowed him to lay down and lean his head on her lap. She stroked his rain-smeared mop with genuine fondness. She didn't care nor complain about the grease of his hair that came off in her hands, she rubbed his hair back nonetheless.

She let him in her bed and kept her arm around his waist as he cried himself to sleep, never questioning or contesting his need for her help.

It didn't mean anything more than a moment of comfort to either of them. Eddie was the only person in the world who knew that he wasn't the gender she fancied. It was more than that. It was a silent, mutual understanding that they had an unspoken knowledge of each other's predicaments.

They were outsiders, but they were outsiders together. In Jenny, Eddie found the family he needed. He found the sister he had lost.

1991

CHAPTER FOUR

*D*erek was so excited he could barely keep his thesis still. Years of study, hard work and, at times, extreme controversy, were summed up in a wad of paper between his fingers.

The Relation Between Demonology Theory and the Evil in Modern Europe Today. A 119,000-word document containing research, experimentation notes, evidence, his hypotheses, first-person accounts; all together in a fascinating piece of reading he was hoping his mentor would be thrilled with.

When he first said he wanted to research parapsychology for his thesis, they had laughed, claiming there was no such area of study; not really, anyway. Now he was stood there, outside the university doors, with the result of his PhD in his hands, having explored the correlation of real-life psychological trauma and the paranormal.

As he filled in the cover form, Jonathon Kume walked over to him and gave him a grand pat on his back.

"Well, this is it, is it?" he smirked, feasting his eyes upon the ring-bound piece of printed beside Derek.

"Yes, sir, it is," Derek smirked back.

"I read the version you sent me, went through it all in one night… fascinating. Truly fascinating stuff."

"Really?"

"Yes. I mean, I won't lie to you, at first I read it out of sheer curiosity. But the empirical evidence you have put forward and the depth into which you go, it's spellbinding stuff."

"Mr Kume, honestly, I…" He was speechless. He opened his mouth and audibly fidgeted around his words. The dean of the university was standing in front of him, endorsing the research that had initially been labelled 'ridiculous hippy bullshit.'

"I can't believe you even read it, never mind appreciated it; it means so much."

"In fact, do you have a minute?" He opened his office door and gestured Derek inside.

"Of course, Mr Kume, of course I have a minute."

"Please, call me Jonathon. It makes sense, seeing as we are going to be working together."

Derek's face turned to utter confusion as he slowly lowered himself to the seat. Jonathon made his way to his side of the desk and aimed a knowing smirk in Derek's direction.

"Whatever do you mean?"

"Derek, I want to fund you and your research."

"Really? You mean you want me to do some tutoring here?"

"Not just tutoring. I want you to set up your own parapsychology department. We will offer it as a course; limited numbers in the first year of course, just as we get it off the ground. You will be able to employ someone else to help carry out your research, and will be eligible to apply for grants, same way any other department is."

Derek could barely move, yet was tirelessly giddy at the same time. He was rooted to the spot, yet shaking with delight. His own department? His own students? Funding for his own research? It was beyond a dream, beyond what he had ever aspired to.

"I was just so fascinated with your research, Derek, and I want to see what else you can find. Assuming you're on board, yes?"

"Why, of course! Not even a question! I can't believe this, Mr Kume, I –"

"Jonathon."

"Jonathon, sorry. I can't believe this."

Jonathon held out his hand and Derek took it firmly, grasping it in a confident handshake.

"It's a pleasure, Derek. An absolute pleasure."

CHAPTER FIVE

*E*ddie could see the perspiration dripping down Jenny's forehead. He squeezed her hand in his.

"Relax," he urged her, so quietly only they could hear. He smiled at her, but she couldn't bring herself to reciprocate. Her look was full of dread, her eyes conveying nothing but worry. He noticed her leg shaking, so he put his hand on it, trying to steady it.

Her parents came into the living room with a tray and gave Eddie his cup of tea, and Jenny her black coffee with three sugars.

"There you go," her mother spoke gleefully, a smile planted across her face. She reckoned she knew what this was about. She took her place next to Jenny's father and sat on the edge of the seat in anticipation.

"Well?"

Eddie glanced at Jenny and saw her struggling to find the words. She began to stutter, then looked to the ground and avoided eye contact.

"Jenny has some news she wants to tell you," Eddie said.

"And it's something I'm really proud of, and she — we — are hoping you will be too."

"You're a couple!" the mother declared, clapping her hands together, bursting it out as if she couldn't hold it in. "We are so pleased for you. We said it, didn't we say it?" She prodded Jenny's father, who wasn't able to get a word in. "Ever since you've been staying here you've been such a calming influence on her, Eddie, and we couldn't be more thrilled."

"No." Eddie shook his head, blushing. "No, that's not what it is."

On another occasion, he may have found this hilarious; he may have sniggered uncontrollably and told the tale for years. But not this time. It was just too awkward.

"Me and Jenny aren't together," Eddie said. "Unfortunately, because of reasons you're about to find out, that would never happen."

"You've found someone else? Whoever it is, surely he isn't as right for you as Eddie?"

"Please." Eddie closed his eyes and lowered his voice, trying to make himself sound calm. "Please, would you just let her speak?"

Her mother realised what she was doing and nodded, faking a smile.

"Very well," she confirmed, and turned her head to Jenny. "Jenny?"

Jenny sighed and closed her eyes. She directed her face away from her parents. She took in a big, deep breath, kept her eyes focused on the corner of the room, and let the breath out.

"I'm gay."

Silence. A hush so tense Eddie started fidgeting, shooting looks between Jenny and her stunned parents.

Jenny looked up at the mother. She needed to see a reaction. She needed to know what look was on her parents' faces.

Then she wished she'd just kept staring at the corner of the room.

Her mother was still poised on the edge of the sofa, but not with anticipation; instead, she was frozen there with shock. Tears were accumulating in the corners of her eyes, and whilst she was clearly fighting them, they were still there nonetheless.

Her father sat back in the chair, away from his wife. He looked emotionless. Whilst her mother was staring solemnly at Jenny with a face of hurt, her father was looking away, staring gormlessly at the arm of the sofa, forcing his face to remain vacant.

Jenny urged them to speak. She willed them to say something, wished they would just respond. She became envious of the rapid-speaking enthusiasm her mother had shown, just moments ago.

"You're…" her Mother tried, but as she went to speak, nothing came out, and her mouth kept moving like a demented duck.

"She's a lesbian," Eddie interjected boldly and confidently. "And I am so proud of her for having the strength to finally be honest with herself, and with others."

He prayed her parents would agree. He knew how much this meant to her, how much she required their approval. What they did in these moments were vital, and something Jenny would remember forever. He was afraid they were abusing that.

Despite giving them the opportunity to agree with him, to say something positive, to reassure her and break her out of the despair they were causing, they didn't. They just sat there, in the same positions, unmoved.

"Can't you… not be?" her mother finally spoke.

Jenny's eyes filled with tears and she fled out of the room, covering her face. You could hear her sobs growing vaguely distant as she stormed through the corridor, ending with the slam of the door.

"I hope you're happy," Eddie spat as he followed. He marched through the hall, out of the front door, and found Jenny rocking back and forth on an aged, rusty swing set. She made no effort to cover her tears. She never needed to, not in front of Eddie.

Eddie perched on the swing next to her, gazing above him at the evening sky. It was chilly, and the hairs on his arms stood on end. He was crying now, hurt at seeing Jenny so distraught, and even more hurt at knowing there was nothing he could do about it. The cold air made his tears harsher on his face and he wiped them away with the shoulder of his t-shirt.

"I'm sorry," he offered. He knew *how are you?* wouldn't cut it, nor would *well that sucks.* It was a situation she was so desperate to go well and he knew how much it meant to her.

She gave him a vague smile of acknowledgement. Her tears subsided and she stared at the ground.

"I really didn't think it would go like that," Eddie admitted. He wasn't lying, he really didn't.

"Me neither," she concurred, not breaking her stare or changing the tone of her voice.

"I still love you." He smiled, this time genuinely. "I know that isn't the same, and it doesn't amount to much, but... it's true."

She nodded. He reached his hand across to her and stroked her hair. With how close they were, he wasn't surprised her mother had thought they were together. It was likely most people did. But in truth, he loved her like a sister. Like the way he had loved his sister before.

"Don't worry, we're going to amount to so much more than them," Eddie announced.

"Sure," she snorted.

"No, we are," he urged. "I mean, what do they do? Some

dead-end job? Forget about it. We are going to do amazing things. I mean that."

"I'm not so sure."

"Yeah we are. I'm going to get a job that will save millions and change lives. You're going to, I dunno, become some activist for gay rights. And we are going to stick together through all of it."

"An activist for gay rights?"

"Okay, maybe not… a teacher then. Or a doctor. Or something that matters. And when that happens, they are going to rue the day they didn't respect you."

Jenny nodded, gazing in his eyes. She really did love him.

"You're so sure, huh?"

"No doubt in my mind."

"Sounds great… though to be honest, I really would just settle with my parents accepting me for who I am."

Eddie pulled her swing closer, put his arms around her, and held her tightly.

"I know."

1995

CHAPTER SIX

*E*ddie awoke and instinctively hit an irritating twitch on his face. He looked at the hand he had just swiped himself with and saw ants. He started hitting his face harder, wiping them away, before looking down and realising his face was resting against an ant hill.

He leant up and surveyed the area. He was on the lawn, with a door to the house left open behind him.

"Damn it," he muttered. He clambered onto his knees and shook his head. Before he could sneak back to his bed, Jenny appeared in the doorway with a huge smirk across her face.

"Sleep-walking again?" she asked, wearing nothing but a shirt that glided off the curves of her body.

"Looks like it." He stood, bashing the dirt off his hands and ants off his cheek. Still, his palms remained covered in soil, so he rubbed them against his pyjama shorts; an item of clothing he was glad he chose to wear last night, considering where he woke up.

Lacy appeared behind Jenny, slipping her arms around her girlfriend's waist and giving her a gentle kiss on the cheek. As soon as she saw Eddie gathering himself in the front garden, she chuckled uncontrollably.

"Yeah, yeah…" Eddie wobbled drearily back into the house and sat himself down in the kitchen.

"Don't know how you did it," Jenny declared, locking the front door and following Eddie into the kitchen, her hand in Lacy's. "We had it locked, bolted, everything. How you manage to do that in your sleep…"

Eddie pretended to ignore the ridicule as he poured Coco-Pops into his bowl to find a mere spoonful come falling out.

"Why don't we have any Coco-Pops?"

"We?" Jenny shot him an inquisitive look.

"Perhaps you can diss *our* cereal choices when it's us sleeping on *your* sofa-bed every night," Lacy backed her partner up. "Speaking of which, not that I know living with lesbians is probably every guy's deepest fantasy, but we have just moved in together. And you're kinda shitting on that. When are you getting a job and your own place?"

Jenny and Lacy both shot him the same look. He was used to that look. He grew up with that look. He remembered when they were sixteen years old, suggesting to Jenny they should nick a few beers from the mini-fridge hidden in her dad's garage. It was the same look she had in 1989 that she had now in 1995, and somehow, since meeting her girlfriend a year ago, Lacy had also managed to perfect the same look.

He sighed and ran his hands through his hair. He repressed a fart, feeling that an unwelcome guest should not release such a thing.

"Seriously, guys, of all days, why today?" he said.

They both looked away uncomfortably. Their breakfast was eaten in silence.

* * *

THE RAIN HIT Eddie's skin hard, falling down his brow and obstructing his vision. He rubbed his eyes, adamantly pushing the water away. He wasn't going to let the rain deter him. Not today.

Putting up his hood so as to avoid the weather that attacked him so violently, he slipped his hands into his pockets and traipsed down the path. He knew the route well. Half-way down the path and four graves to his left. That was where he stopped and knelt.

He stroked his hand down the tombstone.

CASSY KING
GONE BUT NOT FORGOTTEN
1976-1984

A TEAR FELL into the corner of his eye before being lost in the rain. He closed his eyes and bowed his head. He took a moment of silence.

A moment of silence was never enough.

He lifted a stale flower being destroyed by pelting water and crushed it in his hand. He pictured what she would look like now. She'd have long, auburn hair that would have accentuated her petite size and cute facial features. She would have been beautiful. Scrap that; she would have been stunning. A knockout.

Now she was just ashes. Dust in your hand.

He felt responsible. He felt guilty. He was the one chasing her on the bike. He was the one who encouraged her to go faster. So much so that when he finally realised what could happen, his words were lost in the wind and it was too late.

Eleven years without her. Eleven years that ruined his

adolescence, tore apart his family, and left him with an empty space. Eleven years in which he had become a twenty-year-old with no home and a shitty, meaningless job.

Not only could her life have ended up different, so could his.

After glancing at his watch, he understood his time was up. Another year gone by; another year without her. Time for his doctor's appointment. Time to put on a brave face.

Time to put on the mask the rest of the world saw.

CHAPTER SEVEN

*E*ddie perched on the edge of the chair. With every passing year would come the annual renewal of his antidepressants, and it was always coincided with the anniversary of his sister's death. The nurse would check his blood pressure, listen to his heart, and talk monotonously at him before signing him off on another year of emotion-killing pills.

It's amazing how they always remember my name, he contemplated, before realising it would appear on the computer screen.

The point of this repetitive check-up was lost on him. What would be the worst that could happen if his blood or heart was affected? He died? So what? Death would be a welcome friend he would greet with a pat on the back.

"And how are you feeling in yourself, Eddie?"

"Oh, fine, Doctor," he lied, knowing if he said anything different they would likely section him, or increase his medication. As much as he hated his many emotions, he still wanted to feel some of them, and if they upped his dose of Prozac any further it would likely numb him completely.

Although, maybe it would be nice, to not feel... To feel no

37

shame about living on his friend's sofa, no sense of loss for his missing sister, no persistent loneliness playing on his mind night after night.

He trudged away from the health centre, prescription in hand. The rain had subsided and the sun attempted to poke between two stingy clouds, almost as if it was Cassy trying to shine a light on him. He hadn't even started his day at work and already he was soaked through. His hair dripped down his face, and his shirt and trousers were heavy with damp.

His foot had barely placed itself over the threshold of the office when his boss, Larry, requested his presence. Larry stood by his office door with a stance he thought was so authoritative; with his arms folded, and one hand rested on the underside of his chin. He watched over his office of worker bees, appearing convinced that he was the big man overseeing a group of people who thought he was a God — in truth, they all thought he was an arsehole.

"Take a seat, Eddie, Edmuno, the Edatron," Larry said as Eddie dragged his feet through the office door and onto the wooden chair opposite Larry's desk. Larry sat back in his large, no-expense-spared, leather office seat.

Eddie looked around the office. Trophies adorned the shelves, but no pictures of family. Eddie peered at the trophy nearest to him; it was for fourth place in a contest at sports day he had won as a child.

"Is it raining outside then, Eddieboy?" Larry enquired, surveying Eddie's dishevelled appearance.

"Mm." Eddie nodded, not quite sure how to dignify such a ridiculous question with an answer.

"Listen, I need to talk to you, Ed. Can I call you Ed?"

Eddie rubbed his sinus, momentarily closing his eyes, assembling the energy to give a shit. "Sure."

"Great, Ed." Larry shifted in his seat, clasping his fingers together and leaning toward Eddie like a bad therapist. "Listen, we are currently going through some major issueromees in the company, as I am sure you are aware. We're all here like, oh man, how are we going to fix this cadoodle? Some major overhauls have had to be endured, in order to keep the company above board. We are losing greens, dosh, brass tacks, and, let's be frank, we are in danger of going under. Undermundo. Underastic. You are aware of this, yes?"

Eddie shrugged. He was sure he'd heard about it at some point, he just hadn't cared. All he could think was *my God, you are such a tool.*

"Great, well, you see, we are having to cut some losses. Snip-snip, Ed, you get me? This involves us having to make some expendable resources expendable. Unfortunately, my friend, you are one of those expendable resources."

"What?" Eddie rubbed his hand over his forehead and through his hair. It felt like Larry was taking forever to get to his point.

"Ed, we are prepared to offer you a redundancy package that we feel is, well, generous. Unfortunately, that is our only option, and we are going to have to part ways. Apologies."

Eddie looked blankly at his boss. He didn't react. He knew, if anyone was going to be sacked, it would be him. He was tempted to shout it out to the whole office, "Hey, guys, guess what? The biggest arsehole here has fired the second-biggest arsehole here!"

But he didn't. Instead, he aimed a gormless stare back at Larry. He didn't move, he didn't blink, he didn't speak. He just zoned out, numbed all emotions, numbed any panic, numbed his mind, and wished he had been given some more of that Prozac after all.

Breaking the awkward silence, Eddie stood, picked up his bag and left. He exited the office, the room, and then the building. He didn't look back.

As he left, he checked his phone. He had a message from

Jenny and Lacy. They had signed up to adopt a child. They knew it wasn't a complete possibility yet, but they had put their name down. Followed by their new house together, one Eddie would not be able to be a part of.

He conveniently dropped his phone on the ground, followed by his bag, and just began running.

CHAPTER EIGHT

*I*t was the bridge Eddie had always imagined ending things on. It was a suspension bridge, adjoining two parts of Bristol. Beneath it was a big drop. If he aimed to the side, he could land on the surface, hopefully on his head, severely damaging his brain and snapping his neck, leaving him deceased for definite.

Or, there was the water directly below him. He couldn't swim, so he would surely drown. He wasn't sure which would be most painless. Either way, it would be over in minutes. Everything, all of it, over, done.

The sweet release he craved gazed back at him. It was at the edge of his fingertips. He was so close; his dry mouth could almost taste the end. The sound of cars motoring behind him grew faint beneath the *boom, boom* of his heart thumping at his chest.

His right foot gently pressed itself against the ledge, feeling it buckle slightly. He climbed up until he hovered on the top of the fence, and beheld the deathly drop below.

He was so close now. Just one movement and that was it, it was done, he would exist no more.

Cars sped past him, a few honking their horns, very few caring enough to stop; though one did. From behind him, he heard a woman shout: "What are you doing?"

He didn't care. He let the words get lost. They couldn't stop him now.

The water was so distant he couldn't even see the ripples. It was surely freezing. If drowning didn't kill him, the cold would.

His eyes closed.

"Stop!" came from a stranger behind him. A man's voice.

Eddie glanced over his shoulder. He didn't get a good look at the person, but he saw a police uniform. The officer was stood a few metres away, reaching his hand out, edging closer with each precariously placed step.

"Stop moving closer!" Eddie cried out.

How on earth had the police arrived already? He had planned to be dead and gone before the police had any chance. They must have been driving past.

"Okay, I'll stop. But you've got to come down from there, son."

Son? He was nobody's son.

He shook his head, taking a deep inhale of breath.

"It's no good. Please don't try to save me. I'm done."

"I'm sure that's not true. Come on, why don't you come on down and we'll talk about it?"

With a longer glance back, he saw the policeman, middle-aged with a moustache, a large crowd of onlookers gathering behind him, watching, hands over their mouths, frozen to the spot, terrified as to what they might see.

"You enjoying what you see?" he shot at them. "You voyeurs, here to watch a man die... You stopped for nothing else!"

"Don't worry about them, worry about me. Just look into my eyes. That's it. What's your name?"

"Eddie."

He turned his head back to the drop and braced himself.

"Eddie. Nice name. How about you just come down off that ledge and we'll talk about things, yeah? See if we can figure out what's troubling you."

"Issue is, Officer… you seem to be under the impression suicide is something to prevent. Something to discourage. For me, it's my way out. It's my salvation."

He turned his head and looked the officer in the eyes.

"For me, it's the best chance I have."

He scrunched his eyes, tightly, breathed in, and pushed the weight of his body forward, allowing gravity to do the rest.

The sounds of the officer shouting: "No!"; the shocked screams of the onlookers; the shake of the fence… it was all lost in the speed of the wind shooting past his ears. He descended in slow motion. He even smiled.

He enjoyed it. The feeling that it was all nearly over.

With a crash as harsh as a blade against the body, he fired into the water and sank further and further down. He made no attempt to thrash out, no attempt to find the surface.

He relaxed his body and let it weaken.

After a minute's rest, he convulsed. His mouth gaped open, searching for oxygen that didn't come. By this time, he couldn't even see the surface of the water above him, let alone get there.

It hurt. It was a stabbing pain that, no matter how much he wheezed inwards, he couldn't fix. The limbs of his body shot in numerous directions, spasming uncontrollably. He felt his arms and his legs lose their function.

Then it went black. He could feel no more.

CHAPTER NINE

*E*ddie's eyes felt as if they were brand-new. His vision lacked focus and his head was in a daze. He rubbed his eyes in hope that this would fix the problem. It didn't. He tried opening his eyes wide, stretching his eye lids apart.

His vision finally returned. He looked to his left, to his right.

He was in a field. The sun was shining, lighting up the clear, blue sky. It was a perfect day. It was hot, but it didn't burn. It was cool, but without a breeze. As he climbed to his feet, he was startled by how light he felt; it was as if gravity was no longer pushing him down, like he could jump up and nothing would pull him back to the ground.

He peered into the distance, and all he could see was green grass and blue sky. There were no trees, no people, no fence, nothing – just fields as far as he could see.

He ran his hands through his hair, pushing strands out of his face. His hair no longer felt like the greasy mess he had let it become; it was soft, clean, and left a pleasant smell of lavender on his fingers.

Edging across the perfectly groomed grass, soft under his

feet, he urged himself to find someone, something, anything that would give him an indication as to where he was.

His memory came back in flickers. The bridge, the police officer, the jump. The last thing he remembered was struggling for oxygen, his body convulsing…

He had done it! He had ended everything. He was dead.

And he was so happy.

Was this heaven?

He remembered this feeling of being so alive, yet having no air passing through him and no beating in his chest; the familiar sensations of lightness, the feeling of resolution, life no longer weighing him down.

"Ahem," a cough came from behind Eddie.

He turned.

An upright man in a white suit checked a few papers on a clipboard. Eddie scoffed at the cliché of it all.

"Of course there's a guy in a white suit."

"Edward King?" the man asked.

Eddie nodded.

"Excellent. Welcome to the next stage."

Eddie grinned. This was it. He was going to find out what it was all about.

"I am going to take you to-" The man stopped mid-sentence, distracted by something on the sheet of paper in front of him. He did a double take, making sure he had read it correctly. His expression turned from pleasure to concern. He leered up at Eddie, a curious repulsion drifting to solemn sympathy. "I do apologise, but it says here that you committed suicide."

"I did."

"Oh. Well, I'm afraid that's an abomination. The misuse of life. I can't grant you entry. Sorry."

The man smiled with empty compassion. Before Eddie could react or comprehend what that meant, he felt all the weight in his body and the anxiety of his mind return as his feet were dragged downwards.

Roots grew from the ground, gripping his ankles, surrounding and encapsulating his legs with vines and weeds.

"What – what's going on?"

It was no good. The man was already looking back through the papers attached to his clipboard.

Eddie was helpless.

He sunk, the roots tugging him further and further downwards.

He thrashed out for something to hold onto, but it was no good. He was steadily being taken, sinking and sinking and sinking and sinking...

He stuck his arm out and grabbed the man's ankle, who flinched away, repulsed, as Eddie was dragged further down.

He drew one final breath before his head was taken under.

As the blue sky faded from above him, he had a feeling that could be the last time he ever saw it.

CHAPTER TEN

*E*ddie hit the ground with a thud.

The bumps and cracks of the stony surface dug into his spine. He no longer felt light, painless, or content.

He felt *everything*.

Every sore memory, every moment of anguish, every illness he had ever suffered, every relative he had ever grieved, all hitting him with one psychological blow.

Following the pain and the emotional torture was the heat, scalding his body. It was intense, humid, musky; his skin was burning. Rubbing his hazy head, he propped himself up and beheld his surroundings.

He was surrounded by mounds of rock and spewing lava. Every mound of rock had another suffering victim, screaming, whimpering, their begging reverberating until it became an almighty crescendo of despair.

If Eddie stayed to the dead centre of his rock, he would likely be safe from the spewing lava. He had a feeling, however, that it wouldn't be that easy.

Straight ahead of him, he saw *her*.

He recognised her instantly. Her face had been etched onto

his mind at eleven years old. He could never forget her. Now there she was, returned to torment, floating on a rock dead ahead of him.

Her long, black, greasy hair dripped in front of her face, barely showing her cracked, faded lips and her yellow, piercing eyes. She wore a long dress that must have once been white, but had since faded to brown, with patches of red he was sure must be blood.

She was staring at him.

"Who are you?" Eddie screamed. This wasn't the salvation his suicide had aimed for.

She didn't reply. She took a step forward, hunched over, her head directed downwards, her demented facial features slightly visible through her soggy black mane.

It's okay, I'm safe on this rock. It's surrounded by lava, she can't get to me, Eddie told himself.

He was wrong.

Once she reached the end of the rock, she placed her bare left foot on top of the lava and allowed her right to follow. Eddie could hear the *tss* of the burning lava inflicting itself upon the soles of her feet, yet she didn't flinch in the slightest. The flames were flicking around her ankles, spewing ash upon them. Still, she didn't react. Still, she walked over the lava toward him.

He collapsed backwards onto his hands, frantically looking around. Noticing a vacant rock behind him, he considered for a moment whether he could jump to it. As if the lava was reacting to his thoughts, it splashed up and ashes landed on his arm, taking with it any hope of survival. The ashes alone caused Eddie such intense pain that he shrieked out for mercy.

He looked back around. She had made it to the next rock over.

He looked everywhere, desperate for some form of restitution; something, somewhere, that could help him escape.

All those familiar feelings he had repressed so well as a child returned. The sense of hopelessness, the loss, the despair.

She took her last step over the lava and shuffled onto Eddie's rock.

Eddie scrunched up into a ball on the floor, entombing his face in his arms, clenching his eyes shut, refusing to accept her close proximity. He wasn't sure what he hoped to achieve by this, but he didn't care. He braced himself for whatever came next.

Her stench grew stronger. He could tell she had crouched down in front of him.

Her fingers pressed against his temple and his head filled with a thousand migraines. He opened his eyes for a moment to see her leant over him.

He took in the stale, yellow teeth or the saliva filled with blood. She grinned as the surface beneath him began to wrap around his chest. He struggled against it but was unable to put up any real kind of fight.

"Eddie..." came the distant voice of a young girl. Eddie recognised it instantly.

It can't be...

Before he could object any further, the soft hand of a young girl traced down his face. His head was bound to the ground but his eyes were not; he strained them and, sure enough, before him was the face of his younger sister, the age at which she died, a face bursting with endless emotion.

"Cassy..." he sobbed, every childhood feeling he had been successfully repressed resurfaced. The love he held for his sister, how protective he was over her, the loss and longing he had endured, the empty pit in his stomach that he could never replace with the alcohol and empty sex he tried to fill it with...

"Eddie..." she cried over him. "Please, please save me..."

"Cassy?"

"Eddie... they are hurting me..."

49

As she climbed over him, her tears dropping onto his face, he glimpsed her body. She was wearing nothing, yet you could see no skin. She was covered in dried blood, old scars, and faded marks. Every piece of her body was bruised or wounded, her eyes were blackened, and her hair was a matted mess of grease and dried scar tissue.

Before he could react, before he could tell her how much he loved her and how much he missed her, she was gone, replaced by the demon with heads of a man, a ravenous bull, and an aggressive ram. He remembered that beast's name. He remembered it clearly.

Balam.

It roared, blood and saliva falling from its jaw.

"I have your sister's soul!" it snarled with terror. "Come take it from me! Take it and claim your place!"

The female beast appeared in front of Eddie's eyes and sank itself into his body. Piece by piece, it placed its hands inside his, its chest inside his, its head inside his.

Every piece of him became consumed by the feeling of loss and emptiness. The thing he had feared when he saw it as a child was now the thing inside of him.

He felt himself lose control in a manic seizure. His body convulsed, and he foamed from his mouth. When the seizure stopped, he looked up.

She was gone.

That's when he awoke.

CHAPTER ELEVEN

*E*ddie's hospital room filled with chaos as doctors and nurses flooded around him. His eyes barely opened, but he could still pick up on the shock in the room. The medical staff were so frantic, so unprepared for the unexpected eventuality that he might need help.

He awoke again later, once the pandemonium was over. Jenny was sitting next to him, his hand in hers, her eyes red and her cheeks damp.

"Eddie? Can you hear me?"

Eddie turned his head to the side. His neck ached as if he hadn't used it for a long time.

"Jenny…?" he mustered. "Where did the doctors go?"

"What doctors, Eddie? You woke up last night, the doctors were in here then, they've all gone now."

"Jesus…" Eddie attempted to sit up, but Jenny pushed him back down and shook her head.

"Be careful, you're still weak."

"Was I asleep all night?"

"All night?" Jenny's eyebrows narrowed and her confusion

became apparent. "Eddie, you've been under for three months. The doctors thought you were braindead."

Braindead? I was braindead?

He could do nothing but gape at her.

Did she say three months?

"What happened?" he asked, his voice weak.

"You don't remember?" Her lip quivered for a moment, and tears accumulated.

"What?"

"Don't you ever do that again, do you hear me?" She jabbed her finger at him. "You are my best friend. I've known you all my life, I can't imagine…"

She turned her face away from Eddie and toward the open door, concealing the look on her face. The light in the corridor went out, then came back on as a nurse walked past.

Eddie closed his eyes and tried to remember. He saw glimpses. He remembered the woman and the three-headed demon… which must have been a dream. The whole scene of spewing lava and lashing fire, it must have been his subconscious.

"How long did you say I've been out?" Eddie asked.

"A few months," Jenny said, keeping her face turned away from him. He couldn't see her expression, only the shaking of her head.

A few months? Had he been dreaming about that vile woman for months? About Balam? About his sister?

A projection of his anxiety, he decided. Just familiar feelings from his experience as a child. An experience he would never want to relive.

"Is my mum here?"

"Well, no, she wouldn't be, would she? She doesn't give a shit. But I'm here." Jenny was clearly angry and not afraid to show it. She spoke with agitation and impatience, whilst doing her best to retain her dignified demeanour. But she couldn't. It broke. And tears fell like bullets.

That's when Eddie remembered.

The bridge. The policeman. The water.

He had jumped.

He had tried to kill himself.

He had done his best to leave this world and somehow he had been saved; despite being against the odds, despite being braindead, despite being attached to life support, he was saved.

If I was braindead, why didn't they turn off the life support? he wondered. Then he realised. Only his blood relatives could do that, and none of them cared enough to attend.

But Jenny had. Jenny had cared enough. She was there.

Eddie reached out a hand. It took him by surprise how weak that arm felt, but he opened his palm and gestured for her hand nonetheless.

Jenny reluctantly unfolded her arms and leant her hand out to reciprocate the gesture. She finally looked at Eddie. It hurt him to see his best friend crying.

"I'm sorry," he told her.

"You bloody well better be," she snapped. "You may not think anybody gives shit, but I am here, and I do give a shit. So don't ever do that to me again, you hear? Don't ever do that to me again!"

He rubbed her hand gently with his thumb, back and forth.

"I won't."

MILLENNIUM NIGHT

CHAPTER TWELVE

"*A*deline, if you can hear me — hold on. Hold on, sweet girl, I'm coming."

The creature of filth bellows with laughter. Objects launch themselves across the room. Eddie instinctively dodges them, scarcely evading a hardback book from clattering him over the head. The curtains rise and retract against a closed window.

"You delusional sack of shit," declares the dirty words from the innocent girl's mouth. "She should have taken you. She should have taken…"

His eyes widen. This is new. He has faced many demons before, yes, but none that knew anything about him and where he came from.

He assumes the creature is bluffing. There is no way it could know who he is.

"Yes, that's right," it speaks in a low, croaky voice, smirking at him. "That's right… Edward… Eddie… Edward King."

"How-" he stutters. "How do you know my name?"

The belts loosely binding the captive girl's hands to the bed-posts soar from the demon's wrists and smack around Eddie's neck. They tighten around his oesophagus, squeezing harder and harder, and he claws at them, doing all he can to remove them.

It is no good. He can't breathe. He gasps helplessly for air that doesn't come.

Adeline's body rises off of the bed. Through his suffocation he acknowledges a feeling of astonishment; he has not seen this before. He has heard vile words of foreign languages spew out of a homeschooled child's mouth; he has seen objects move of their own accord — he has even seen purple vomit float in the air.

But never has he seen a body levitate five feet off the ground.

"How..." he says, but can speak no further. The belts close around his throat, pressing in on his gullet. He becomes faint. He becomes weak.

The demon moves Adeline's body through the room until it hovers vertically in front of Eddie and looks him directly in the eyes.

"Eddie..." it whispers, this time in Adeline's faint, weakened voice.

Eddie reaches his hand into his back pocket and grasps his crucifix. He withdraws it, and lurches himself toward the monster, the crucifix held out in front of him. The demon recoils, enough for it to lose its grip over the belt suffocating his throat, allowing Eddie to rip it away and throw it to the side.

He drops to his knees, takes rapid intakes of breath, and wills himself to regain his senses.

It's funny, really, he tells himself. *Five years ago I'd have laughed at someone who had a crucifix. Now it just saved my life.*

After spending more time than he would like gathering himself, he looks up. It's gone quiet. No slain, battered body stands in front of him. His eyes dart around the room. Then he sees her, in the top right corner of the room. Its limbs dislocated out of their sockets, pressed against the ceiling and the wall to hold the tormentor in place.

"You are to let the girl go, now," he demands, rising to his feet. "In the name of God, you are to let Adeline go."

"In the name of who?" the creature grins.

Objects circle around the room with more vigour and aggression. Paper slaps against his heels and spins around his feet. Broken furniture drags across the floor. Shards of glass nip against his bare skin. Wind batters Eddie's ears, to the point he has to shout to be heard.

"In the name of God, foul creature!" He takes a few steps toward the corner of the room the creature resides in. "I am giving you the chance to leave. Leave, and no harm will come to you!"

"No harm will come to... *me?*"

A large claw mark slits across the girl's chest, splashing blood across the floor. For a moment, Eddie can hear Adeline scream from somewhere inside the body. The creature just smiles.

"I assure you, Eddie" — it pronounces his name with such emphasis it makes him shiver — "it does not do to dwell on the damned... Adeline is gone. And I can do more to harm her than you can do to harm me."

He holds out the crucifix, strengthening his grasp.

"You think that that cross will work again, you thick cunt?" the demon spits. "You used it once to take me by surprise. You've used that trick already."

"Tell me your name," Eddie snarls back.

A mixture of thick, red-and-green vomit spews out of the demon's mouth, like a canister of toxicity unleashed over the remaining, unspoilt remnants of earth, boiling and bubbling through the carpet.

"What is your name? You have taken this girl, you can at least tell us your name! If only to amuse you, you foul beast."

"My name," it chuckles, "is *Balam*."

Eddie stumbles back.

His knees become weak.

It can't be.

1995

CHAPTER THIRTEEN

*E*ddie awoke with a jolt. His face rested against dirt. There was a strange sensation upon his foot.

Realising where he was, he leant up and peered across his body. It was a dog, licking his toes like there was no tomorrow.

"Oy!" came their neighbour, Roger, as he walked past, a middle-aged father with oversized glasses and a bald spot. The dog promptly chased after its owner.

"Hi, Roger!" called out Eddie.

"Morning," Roger replied with a grin, quite used to the sight of Eddie waking up on the lawn.

Eddie peered around for his crutches. How on earth he'd managed to sleep walk to the middle of the front garden with the pain he was in, he did not know. He noticed one crutch laid on the floor a few paces back and one propped against the front door. As he dragged himself along the grass to retrieve his crutches, the door opened and Jenny appeared behind him with a cup of coffee.

Eddie used the crutch to help himself to his feet and limped toward her, grunting as a thank you for the warm, tasty, caffeinated beverage.

"Have a good night last night, Eddie?" she asked with her unique, unmistakable air of sarcasm that Eddie knew too well. The tone of her voice told Eddie that she was unlikely to have had as good a night as he.

"Not sure, don't remember," he replied with honesty. "Why?"

"You can barely walk around your sofa bed without banging your toe on a beer bottle." She stood with her hands on her hips, clearly agitated about her lack of sleep. "We spoke about you moving out and that was delayed and all that after your accident, but if you're going to be a prick about it, you can be gone."

Eddie limped his way past Jenny and into the house. As he passed the sofa bed, he almost choked at the sight of bottles, cans and open crisp packets spread across the floor.

"I'm sorry, Jenny," he told her. "I'll deal with it. I promise. By the time you get home from work..." He trailed off as he stumbled his way into the kitchen and sat at the table. He placed his coffee down and his hood up. Jenny stood behind him with her arms folded, shaking her head, stumped as to what to say to him.

Lacy broke the uncomfortable silence with her chirpy entrance to the room, jokingly pulling his hood down and switching on the kettle. She was wearing tiny pyjama shorts, and Jenny was incensed even further when she spotted Eddie staring at her dainty backside.

"So how's your head today?" asked Lacy, filling her cup of coffee and leaning against the sink, turning her inquisitive gaze toward him. She was a lot more relaxed than Jenny, but Jenny was his oldest friend, and Eddie knew he was letting her down with every day he stayed there, messing up the life they were trying to build as a couple.

"Bad," he answered. "Hey, can anyone drive me to therapy today?"

Jenny scoffed as she loaded Eddie's dishes from the previous night into the sink.

"I can," Lacy interjected, before Jenny could start one of her lectures. "I'm going that way into town, I can drop you off. But you'll need to get the bus back."

"Sure, thanks. Say, you got any change for the bus?"

Jenny dropped the dishes in the sink and stood over them, her arms stiff and her fists clenching. She closed her eyes and gathered her thoughts, urging herself not to jump into a rant.

"How about you get a job, then you can pay for it?" Jenny answered, turning toward him, clutching a mug filled with mould that he had left out for weeks. "I understand you tried to harm yourself, I do. I understand you're on crutches. But welcome to the real world. This is it. And we have to work to make a living."

Lacy walked over to her girlfriend and put an arm around her. Jenny leant her head against Lacy's chest and allowed her to calmly stroke her hair. She always seemed to become calmer when Lacy had her arm around her.

"I'm sorry," Eddie said, attempting to put some emotion into it. "I am. I'll be out of here as soon as possible. Maybe there's a shelter or something."

"Nonsense, Eddie, you are not staying at a shelter," Lacy said, prompting Jenny to slam the mug down into the sink and storm out of the room.

Lacy took a seat opposite Eddie, wrapping her hands around her mug.

"But maybe you should think about contributing something here," she advised. "Or at least cleaning up your shit. I mean, have you seen the living room? It looks like town centre on a Saturday night."

"I know, I know." He shook his head to himself. He did know and he felt like an arse. "I'll do it. Got any bin bags?"

"Under the sink, loser. You don't even know where the bin bags are?"

Eddie laughed. Her voice was playful and bouncy. She was always so happy.

"You know, you're too hot to be a lesbian," he told her, instantly regretting saying something so ill-timed.

"Right, well, don't tell Jenny that, or she will kill you. We leave in ten. Get the crap picked up before then."

She left the room and he sat there, alone. He did know how much Jenny had done for him, and he was grateful —although, admittedly, he could express his gratitude more often. He was sixteen when his family abandoned him, and Jenny's family selflessly took him in. Ever since then she had been his family, and his best friend. Jenny was fantastic, though understandably irritable; he felt bad for putting so much on her.

Reluctantly, he grabbed a bin bag from under the sink, limped his way to the sofa bed, and tidied up his rubbish.

* * *

IT FELT weird to be sat on a couch, spilling his guts to a total stranger who just sat there, writing it all down. Eddie wasn't sure how this was supposed to help him; surely, she should give him some kind of advice? Not just let him ramble on incessantly and self-indulgently...

Was she waiting for him to have an epiphany? Some kind of realisation that meant he wasn't a complete fuck-up anymore?

Well, it hadn't happened yet.

He glanced over her credentials, framed proudly on her desk. Doctor Jane Middlemore, first-class honours degree in clinical psychology, master's in mental health research, PhD in something that looked way too complicated for him to be able to pronounce.

"And your father, you said he's in prison?"

Eddie snapped out of his daze and nodded vacantly. He was tired; even though he'd had a full night's sleep, he had been sleepwalking for most of it.

"And how does that make you feel?"

Eddie shrugged. How did it make him feel? He felt nothing. His father had stopped being his father the day Cassy had died. The caring, loving family man he once was had disappeared, and a sad, cynical, abusive drunk, who spent his time beating on him and his mother, took his place.

There was one Christmas when he was young, when Jenny's parents took him to visit his father in prison. He was able to look at that day with adult's eyes now, and he was able tell they only did it for some kind of closure.

"So what does make you angry, Eddie?"

Eddie shrugged again. What kind of question was that?

"Surely there has to be something?"

"I dunno," he mumbled. "Cats."

"Cats?" she replied.

"Sure. Cats, they piss me off when they shit on the lawn and stuff."

It may not have been the kind of answer she was looking for, but honestly, there had been many mornings when he'd woken up on the lawn after a night of sleepwalking to find himself laying in a lump of cat shit. It had taken him around four rounds of lather, rinse, and repeat to shampoo it completely out of his hair.

"Surely there's something that annoys you more than that? Something to do with your family maybe?"

Oh, who cares?

Honestly, so what if he was annoyed his mother disowned him and his father got put away. What was moaning to some sanctimonious doctor going to do about it?

He gazed out of the window. He could see a playground in the distance. Fathers pushed their children on the swings.

Mothers sat on the bench gossiping. Students played football on the adjoining field. He had never known what it was like to do such things. Was he angry about it? Sure. Did he care enough to show it? Probably not.

In the distance, in the wooded area beyond the playground, he saw something. A figure. A familiar, slouched posture.

Jane peered over her shoulder to see what he was staring at.

"What is it?" she said, but he did not reply. He was transfixed, as if in a hypnotic gaze, and no matter how much she glanced out of the window and back at Eddie, she appeared unable to see what he saw.

But he saw it, alright.

The figure was moving forward with an exaggerated limp, walking disjointedly, staying in the shadows, mixing so completely with its darkness that the contours of its body became barely intelligible. Its hair fell over its face, greasy, black and long. Its eyes were black and deadened, its features scarred and broken.

This figure...

He'd seen it before...

He backed up in his chair, gripping the armrest so hard that tufts of stuffing came out.

Jane peered over her shoulder. She just saw children in the playground.

"What, Eddie? What is it?" she asked.

He couldn't speak.

The terrifying vision of his nightmare, the woman who had appeared to him both as a child and as a man, it was...

It couldn't be...

He had only seen it in his unconscious, yet here she was, standing across the playground as clear as Doctor Jane beside him.

He'd never seen her with his eyes open before.

His legs were numb. All down his body he felt shivering,

coldness, tension. His hands continued to grip the sofa, continued to claw at the armrests.

"Eddie?"

His face turned to horror, his skin turned to ice.

How was she here?

She had only appeared to him when he'd been comatose; how was she here?

What was she after?

Why now?

Why him?

"Eddie?"

Her arm reached out, a stained finger with a broken nail pointing toward him. Her head lifted up, lifting, lifting, her eyes focusing on his.

He didn't blink. He couldn't. He was paralysed.

"Eddie!" Jane shouted.

Eddie abruptly refocused his eyes on her. He snapped out of whatever daze he was in, his head full of mist, confused, derailed.

"Eddie, what were you staring at?"

He turned back to the playground, peering at the wooded area.

She was gone.

Like she'd never been there.

"Eddie, what was it?"

He couldn't speak. He couldn't answer. What would he even say?

Even though he could no longer see her, he felt her near.

Her presence consumed him.

CHAPTER FOURTEEN

*D*erek stepped out of the car, clutching the case report in his hand, and took in the beauty of the old, decrepit manor house that stood before him.

Plaster hung off the walls, the paint had peeled, and windows were engrained with dust, but it was old and unique. Just as you would picture a typical haunted house in a movie, it stood there with plenty of character and plenty of shadows.

Levi stood beside Derek and surveyed the house. He was younger and far scruffier than Derek. Derek prided himself on his tidiness, making sure he was always dressed in a full suit with a top button done up. Levi was much younger and far 'cooler' than he, dressing with a scruffy red t-shirt and baggy jeans with fashionable rips in the knees. Buying jeans with rips in them sounded like a ludicrous idea to Derek, it was like buying a half-eaten apple. Why would you buy something that was already nearly done with?

"Shall I unload the van, like?" he asked.

"Yes, please, Levi," Derek answered, gazing at his notes. Whatever he thought of Levi's fashion sense or youthful sensibilities, he did the job he was employed to do and he did it well.

But, being one of Derek's students, Levi was unaware of the pressure Derek's department was under.

"I employed you because you had a fascinating thesis, and I thought the research was interesting," Jonathon had ranted at him, having called him to his office. "But I see no talking points in your research since, just a load of failed cases and no grounds for what you are able to teach your students. I mean my God, if I wanted to learn about false claims and how to spot a phony, I'd go to church!"

Derek respected Jonathon and knew he was right. His thesis had been an intriguing piece of writing that had gained more attention than he ever thought it would, but he had not provided anything substantial in the three years since. Every case he'd investigated where people had claimed they had evidence for ghosts had been easily explained by other means. He was growing tired. His students weren't getting the insight they had hoped for, and the dean of the university was growing impatient, and with good cause.

But this could be the one. The things this family had said about this house were so fascinating and unlike any case so far. It had to be true.

He reread the notes, written in Levi's scruffy handwriting.

- *Gargling sounds echoed throughout the house every night.*
- *Intermittent flickers of light whenever they walk past.*
- *The cross upon the kitchen wall burnt when touched.*

The list went on.

As Levi brought the equipment into the living room, Derek introduced himself to the family. They were an ordinary family, and their appearance did not match the grandness of the house; a father called Guy who worked in real estate, a mother called Helen who worked part-time as a teaching assistant, and two young daughters: Kaley, five, and Yvonne, eight.

"Do you mind if I look around the house?" Derek said, taking the cup of tea they had offered.

"Yes. We don't leave the living room anymore," the father admitted. "We get sleeping bags and camp out here, we are too scared."

"Tell me, has anyone else been in this house recently?"

"No. We had a plumber here, but that was a few weeks ago."

With a nod, Derek sipped his tea and carried it through the living room. He looked around, listening for noises, feeling for a difference in temperatures, smelling for disgusting odours. He found nothing to note in his initial assessment, but delayed his scepticism until he had been there a little longer.

He walked into the kitchen and spotted the crucifix on the wall above the oven. It was made of metal.

He made his way up the creaking stairs, each step moaning beneath his feet. He reached the top and placed his ear against the wall. He heard a faint gurgling sound, so he stayed still and listened to it for a few minutes.

He passed through the hallway a few times, then made his way back downstairs and returned to the living room. He passed the fuse box on the way, and stopped to fiddle with a few of the switches. One of the switches fell off and he put it in his pocket.

He closed the living room door behind him, looked at the faces of the each terrified family member in turn, then turned to Levi, who was unpacking the equipment.

"Levi, sorry to be a pain, but please, could you stop unpacking and put all of the equipment back in the van?"

"What? Are you kidding? I just got it all out."

"I know, and I do apologise, but I'm afraid we won't be needing it."

With an huff, Levi shoved the bits and pieces back inside the boxes and began heaving them back to the rear of the van.

"What's going on?" the father, Guy, enquired.

"You said there was a fault with the electricity going on and off?"

"Yes, it keeps flickering."

"Tell me, was it mainly the hallway landing?"

"Yes!"

Derek took the fuse switch out of his pocket and presented it in his hand.

"This is the fuse switch for the hallway light. It came off when I touched it. It has been loose for a while, I would reckon?"

"I guess…"

"That means that it isn't secure and it keeps turning the fuse off at random times. You said your crucifix burnt in your hand?"

"Yes, every time, we can't even touch it anymore."

Derek smiled and rubbed his sinus. Another case of clear explanations.

"That is because you have it above the oven and it is on a metal base. Metal conducts heat, therefore every time you cook, you are making the metal hotter."

"But what about the gargling sounds? Throughout the whole house?"

"Tell me, this plumber who was here a few weeks ago. Was he from an independent business? A small one?"

"Yes, yes he was… Byson or something."

"Drison – the company is the same as its owner's last name."

Derek fumbled in his bag and took out a newspaper report, handing it to Guy. The headline read: *Drison Plumbing Company shut down after record number of complaints.*

"You weren't the only one to report gargling and you weren't the only one who used this plumbing company."

"Oh." Guy's mouth dropped as he skimmed the article.

"Have a good day," Derek said before anyone could object. He left the house and made his way hastily to the passenger seat of the van.

"What is it?" Levi enquired.

"Another waste of time, Levi. Another bloody waste of time."

CHAPTER FIFTEEN

*J*ane sat across from Eddie, resting a cup of tea on her lap. Devil horns protruded from her forehead. Eddie wasn't sure why. He was sitting in her office, wearing a suit. He never wore a suit. He couldn't understand where it had come from.

"Do you see her, Eddie? Do you see her?" Jane kept repeating, over and over. "Do you see her, Eddie? Do you see her?"

"Do I see who? I don't understand; do I see who?"

She smiled and continued to ask, "Do you see *her*, Eddie? Do you see *her*?"

Then, as if by cue, the dark figure he had come to dread rose from behind her. It stood over her. Jane was laughing; no, it was more than just laughter — she was guffawing hysterically.

"I am here in Balam's name," the figure spoke.

The dark figure grew and grew and grew, ominously lurching over him. As its jaw extended to the length of its body and moved toward him, he screamed a deafening scream.

"Holy shit, Eddie, wake up!"

Eddie's eyes opened with a start. He jolted upright, looking around. He was on the sofa bed. In Jenny and Lacy's house. A blanket loosely draped over him, his pyjama shorts sticking to him through sweat. Jenny stood over him.

"Jesus, Eddie," she exclaimed. "You were screaming."

"I – I had a bad dream," he stuttered, still gathering his thoughts, still taking in what had happened. He was awake and safe. It wasn't real.

But she was there. She was always there.

"Coffee, Eddie?" Jenny asked, giving him a perturbed glance and walking into the kitchen. Eddie followed her in and sat at the table, opposite Lacy, who was already half-way through her Bran Flakes covered in pieces of banana. Eddie groaned at the sight of her breakfast. He didn't know how she could eat that stuff.

Jenny placed a coffee in front of Eddie.

"So what was the dream about?"

Eddie ran his hands over his face and through his hair. He really didn't want to have to relive it. It would take so much explanation, which he was not ready for. He didn't want to have to face the questions: who was this woman? Why did he keep seeing her? Why was she in his dreams? All questions he didn't have an answer for.

"I don't remember," he lied, sipping on his coffee.

"You're sweating like crazy, it must have been bad."

"I honestly don't know."

He wiped a thick layer of perspiration from his forehead. He'd grown so used to waking up to a hangover he had almost forgotten what it was like to wake up without a headache.

"Well, don't forget, it's my nephew's christening today, and you're coming with me."

Eddie bowed his head. He had forgotten. "Why can't Lacy go?" he moaned.

"Because I have class, you ball of sunshine!" Lacy joked,

always bringing a happy edge to whatever tension was between him and Jenny.

Eddie took Lacy's laptop from the seat beside him. "Mind if I use this for five minutes?" he asked.

"Sure."

He opened Internet Explorer and loaded Google. He'd had enough of these dreams, these visions, whatever they were. He so adamantly didn't believe in this stuff, yet there was a niggling doubt in his mind that everything going on inside his head, everything that was tormenting him, was true. That the image of his sister he had seen when in a coma was not fake.

He shook his head. He'd considered himself to be a rational human being. It was absurd.

He typed *Balam* into Google and straight away an article came up. He clicked on it and read:

In demonology, Balam (also Balaam, Balan) is a great and powerful king (to some authors a duke or a prince) of Hell who commands over forty legions of demons.

Balam is depicted as three-headed. One head is the head of a bull, the second of a man, and the third of a ram. He has flaming eyes and the tail of a serpent. At other times he is represented as a naked man riding a bear.

THREE HEADED — the head of a bull, man, and ram. Riding a bear. It was so familiar. It was exactly what he'd seen. It had stood before him, holding onto his sister.

Yet he had never heard of this demon before. How could his mind have been so accurate on something he knew nothing about?

And why on earth would a king of hell be interested in him anyway?

Ludicrous.

"Come on, you need to get your suit on. We leave in half an hour."

He leant his head back and closed his eyes. He could not think of anything worse than going to a christening. He had been friends with Jenny for so long that her family all thought of him as family, and it would be expected of him to go, but the whole thing felt like an initiation into a cult to him. He despised religion, and he despised the process of indoctrinating a young child into something they were not old enough to understand yet.

"I'll be ready," he grunted, rising from his chair and heading into the living room to change, coffee in hand.

* * *

JENNY GLANCED at Eddie in the passenger seat beside her. He would actually be quite good-looking if he took care of himself. As it was, his hair was a mess, his facial hair unkempt, and his tidy suit looked like a poorly-fitted, scruffy mess.

She pulled up in the church car park and they stepped out of the car. Eddie flinched at the sun. He normally sat at home in front of day-time television all day; he wasn't used to the light. Wondering what the theme on Jerry Springer was that afternoon, and regretting that he was missing it, he followed Jenny into the church and greeted her family.

He shook hands with Jenny's parents, her sister (and mother of the boy getting christened), and their family friends. He knew these people better than his own parents, or even his foster parents. He had spent most of his adolescence in a sleeping bag on their living room floor, or hanging around for their family film nights, not to mention when he lived with them for two years from the age of sixteen. It was the closest thing he'd ever had to a family life.

He stood at the back, his arms folded, squinting at the light and staring at the crowd gathered around the altar. The vicar held the helpless baby over the water, as Jenny and the other godparent stood on either side.

"Do you promise to guide this child on his voyage to God?" the vicar asked.

"I do," Jenny replied. Eddie scoffed. These were the people Jenny had concealed her sexuality from for so long. The church had been so negative about it, he was surprised they were even letting her do this. Then it occurred to him that the vicar probably didn't even know. He wondered what would happen if he was to blurt the information out.

"Will you pray for him, draw him by your example into the community of faith and walk with him in the way of Christ?"

"I will."

Eddie turned away, covered his eyes and exhaled as he contemplated how much he detested this. When he turned back, the vicar was staring at him.

The vicar didn't move. He was rooted to the spot, the baby held midair, his eyes fixed on Eddie.

Eddie looked around to see if it was someone else that he was staring at. Sure enough, he was the only one in the vicar's eye line. Everyone else began staring too, looking between Eddie and the vicar like a tennis match, confused as to why the vicar had abruptly paused the service to stare at this random man. Nobody knew what was going on.

Eddie became uncomfortable. "What?" he whispered, barely able to get his words out. He did not like having this attention.

"Is everything okay, Vicar?" asked Jenny. The vicar slowly handed the baby to her, not taking his eyes from Eddie for a moment. He ambled from behind the altar, and the congregation moved aside to allow a clear path between Eddie and him.

"What?" Eddie begged. "I really don't know what's going on."

With sudden speed, the vicar marched toward Eddie and stood directly in front of him. He reached his hand out and placed it on Eddie's heart, his eyes widening and his lip raised in a sneer. His face turned red as his body shook.

"You..." he muttered.

"What?" Eddie asked, desperate for an answer. He had kept all those thoughts inside his head, hadn't he?

"You..." the vicar snarled. "Are not welcome here."

Eddie frowned. He looked around, hoping someone would make some kind of sense of this. No one spoke. Everyone just stared, either out of awkwardness or fear.

"Don't look at them for help!" the vicar said, inches from Eddie's face. "They won't help you! They are all God's children. You, you foul wench, you are not welcome here."

"I don't know what you are talking ab-"

"Out! Out!" The vicar nudged Eddie toward the door. "Be gone!"

Eddie glanced at Jenny and shrugged his shoulders. She shook her head; another family event, another wreckage by Eddie.

Once Eddie had finally been ushered beyond the threshold of the church, he stood there, staring at the vicar, so confused.

"And don't ever come back!" the vicar shouted, slamming the door shut in front of him.

A few passers-by looked at him and he glanced back awkwardly. He had no idea what had happened. Did the vicar just call him a foul wench?

All he knew was that there was something more to what was happening than he understood.

MILLENNIUM NIGHT

CHAPTER SIXTEEN

*E*ddie rests his head against the wall and lets out a long sigh. His legs ache, perspiration drips down his forehead, and his heart beats harder than he can take.

The creature simply rests on the ceiling above, laughing. Cackling at Eddie's misfortune. Laughing at the no-hope, defeated fool that sits beneath it.

"Give up yet?" it says, in a voice far too deep and sinister to be coming out of the body of a teenage girl.

Eddie closes his eyes and attempts to calm his breathing down. He disregards the demon's taunts; rising to them only fuels the arrogance of this sadistic beast. He is up against it and he knows it more now than ever.

He has been fighting this demon for longer than he is aware of.

"I will not be giving up today," he mutters, assuring himself more than his opponent. "You can do all you wish to me, I will not leave until I have cast you out of Adeline's body and freed my sister's soul."

It booms a deep, grand laugh that echoes against the walls. It peels itself off the ceiling and floats in the air above him.

Items fly around it in a whirlwind: rubbish, paper, fluids — everything in the room is off the floor and floating. The bed rattles and the windows open and shut furiously.

Eddie rises to his knees. Ignores the ache in his muscles. Wills himself to be stronger. He cannot let this thing win, no matter what it costs him.

"The eve of the new millennium," he says. "It was said that today would be the day Hell would attempt to rain down upon us. So many people are waiting for the second coming of Christ that they aren't even aware of the coming of you."

He spits the final 'you' at the demon through gritted teeth. He fills with hatred. This is the thing besieging the form of this innocent girl.

This is the entity imprisoning his dear, dead, chastised sister.

"And you are the one to stop me?" taunts the demon.

"Yes, I am."

"And why you, Edward King?"

Eddie bows his head, calms himself, clenches his fists, then lifts his head again — renewed, prepared.

"Because I have the sight. That is why you are after me, is it not?"

The demon doesn't answer.

"And you're Balam, huh?"

The demon nods, and gives a little bow.

"You are Balam?" Eddie continues. "A great and powerful king of hell, commanding over forty legions of demons. You are three-headed, are you not? A head of a bull, a man and a ram. Flaming eyes and tail of a serpent. Balam, the biblical magician."

"The very one," smiles the demon.

"You are a ruler in Hell. Demons are petty thieves who take over people's bodies, but you are a ruler of demons. Why on earth would you bother taking one of our girls?"

The creature just smiles. The face of a girl, the mind of the despicable. Eddie puts on a strong façade, but inside, he is cowering.

"Where is my sister?"

Laughter. *More damn laughter.*

"I said, where is my sister?"

"Are you forgetting about how you need to save poor Adeline?"

"Then you do not have her soul. I have freed her."

Laughter turns to a knowing grin. It incenses Eddie.

Enough.

He produces a flask of holy water and splashes it over the demon. It flinches. The sound of burning and singeing arises from Adeline's skin.

"Let this girl go!" Eddie demands. "Let this child of God return to her rightful body. Be gone, beast!"

He plants his foot against the wall and gives himself a push up, using the force to leap onto Balam. He brings the demon down and slams it against the floor, mounting it. He produces a crucifix and presses it against the face of the creature; harder and harder, until it writhes in pain.

"The power of Christ compels you! The power of God compels you!" His eyes narrow. "*I* compel you!"

The demon closes its eyes and breathes in through its nose, soaking up the hostility of its opponent. It holds its arms out and begins to rise. Eddie remains balanced upon its torso as it levitates in midair. Eddie tries to stay still, to not fall off. If he gets knocked unconscious, God knows what the demon would do to him then.

It flings Adeline's eyelids open to reveal two eyeballs of complete white. In that white, Eddie sees fire — flames where a pupil should be.

"You do not scare me, beast!"

With a loud scream, in which Eddie is sure he can hear

multiple voices, the beast sails across the room and halts beside a wall, sending Eddie flying into the wall and onto the floor.

He feels his forehead. He's bleeding. He clambers to his knees, shaking away the dizziness.

The demon sits on the edge of the bed, watching, waiting. It taps its foot and drums its hand on its knee. "Having some trouble?" it enquires.

Eddie lifts his head and brushes a strand of sweaty hair out of his eye. He dabs his lip, feeling a cut. He licks his lip with his tongue as he stands. He sets his feet shoulder-width apart, straightens his legs, and regains his perfect posture.

"Adeline, I am talking directly to you now."

"Adeline isn't here…"

"You need to be tough. I know it's hard, but you need to fight too. It's no good just me fighting from the outside; you've got to fight from the inside. I know you can, girl, because you're strong. I can still feel you there, so you're strong."

"You're a fool."

1995

CHAPTER SEVENTEEN

*E*ddie stood on the porch, unable to believe what he was about to do. A wind-chime floated in the breeze above him and numerous cats brushed against his ankles. The door was cracked and covered in vines. He rubbed some sleep out of his eyes and knocked.

"Enter," came a voice from inside. He pulled his hand out of his pocket and pushed the door open. It creaked. He stepped inside and shut the door behind him.

In front of him was a grand set of marble stairs. To his left, a large living room, and to his right, what he assumed was the kitchen. Against the walls were bookcases covered in dust, with tattered, plain-covered books. Eddie picked out a few titles as he walked past: *History of the Occult, Manipulating the Elements, Intermediate Tarot Reading.*

"In here," came a voice to his left. He turned and approached the living room cautiously. He admired all of the various ornaments as he entered. There was pottery, paintings older than Eddie could imagine of people who were probably long gone, and a few mirrors with large, gold frames.

He edged past a ripped armchair that looked like it was created in the 1920s, and over the dusty, fluff-ridden carpet. Sitting at a rickety, wooden table before him was a woman, smiling.

"Eddie?" she asked. He nodded. She held her hand to indicate the seat opposite her. He placed himself down and sat awkwardly on the edge of the chair.

She was a rather weighty woman with her hair tucked back in some kind of purple cloth. Her red-and-purple gown hung low off her arms and her body, and her fingers were far bigger than they needed to be. Every time she spoke, Eddie couldn't help but notice the wattle underneath her chin shaking.

"I don't really know what I'm doing here," he admitted. "I'm an atheist."

"Most don't," she said. "But there must be a reason you wish to see me."

"There is…" he began and trailed off. He hadn't even started to think about how he was going to put this into words. "There's a woman. She looks — she has black hair, scarred skin. She's been following me around since I was a child."

"Since you were a child, you say?"

"I saw her when I was in a coma as a kid, then again in a coma a few months ago. Then, I saw…"

He thought of Cassy, her tearful eyes, and the scars over her body.

"In a coma again?"

"Huh? Oh, yes. And then I said her again. Outside my therapist's window. Pointing at me."

She studied him carefully, and considered up every word he said. She seemed like she was trying to emulate an air of wisdom, but it all felt fabricated.

"Take my hands, Eddie," she instructed, and lifted her hands out. With reluctance, Eddie withdrew his hands from his lap and placed them in hers.

"What I'm going to do now," she explained, "is read you. I'm going to look at your past, your present, and your future."

Eddie nodded, not completely sure what she was on about.

"It is essential — no, it is *crucial* — that you do not let go of my hands. Whatever happens. Understood?"

Eddie nodded.

"It is imperative that you acknowledge this."

"Yeah, fine, I won't."

"Okay, we shall begin."

She closed her eyes and wriggled in her chair, getting comfortable. Then she went quiet. Eddie watched her. She just sat there, her eyes closed, completely still. He wasn't sure what to expect, but he would have thought she would do something more than sit opposite him with her eyes closed and his hands in hers.

He looked around, his eyes wandering out of boredom. He noticed a few more paintings around the house, some antlers off a dead animal, another grand sculpture of–

"Eeeeuuuurrrrggghhhh."

Eddie almost jumped out of his skin. He stared at her peculiarly. Had she just made that sound?

"Aaaaaarrggghhh."

Her eyelids flickered and her head began to shake.

The lights flashed. Eddie looked around. Had he just seen that? The lights went dim, then on, he was sure of it. Or had he imagined it?

In an abrupt movement, the psychic's neck straightened and she faced directly upwards.

She screamed. A large, manic scream.

"Are you okay?" Eddie whispered.

Her head clamped back into position, facing straight ahead. Her eyes remained completely closed. But she was shaking. Vibrating, like boiling water, waving Eddie's hands pugnaciously from side to side. It became more and more violent until her whole body was jerking in a seizure.

Eddie tried to withdraw his hands. He knew he was told not to, but this was too much.

But it was no good. Her hands gripped his so hard that he couldn't get out, however much he wanted to.

"Wake up!" he shouted, pulling his hands back, attempting to get them loose.

Eventually, he managed to jerk himself completely out of her grip and fell flat out on his arse. She backed up into the corner of the room, staring at him. Her eyes were wide and her expression was one of complete, stiff terror and bewilderment.

"What?" Eddie asked, feeling like it was a stupid question.

"I..." She tried to speak, but could barely move. "I... can't help you..."

She turned away and buried herself into the corner of the room, shoving her face in her hands and crying. She was rapidly shaking her head, repeating, "No, no, no, no."

Eddie got to his feet and backed up to the door, deciding this was a good time to go.

"Wait!"

Eddie froze.

She grabbed a piece of paper from a dresser next to her, wrote down a number, and edged toward him. She reached the note out, keeping a safe distance. Once he had taken it, she backed up again.

"That's the number of a paranormal investigator, maybe he can help you," she spoke, her eyes still transfixed on him. "But I can't. Sorry, child, but I can't... May God be with you."

With the last, sincere five words she spoke to him, she darted out of the room, and Eddie could hear her feet stomping as she rushed upstairs.

Eddie looked at the note. It had a phone number and a

name: *Derek Lansdale, Ph.D., Paranormal Investigator.* Why had she handed him a number for a paranormal investigator? And what had she seen that had freaked her out so much?

Telling himself it was all an act, he walked out of the house, stuffing the number into his back pocket.

CHAPTER EIGHTEEN

*E*ddie lay wide awake, gazing at the ceiling. He hadn't called the paranormal investigator; the piece of paper was still slotted into the back pocket of his jeans, untouched. He'd spent the last few days considering calling them, but couldn't bring himself to do it. Every time he picked up the phone, he reminded himself he didn't believe in that stuff. He was an atheist. Despite what monstrosities his mind had shown him, he was still a rational person who did not let himself get drawn into ridiculous claims.

But there was still that niggling thought at the back of his mind, the thought that reminded him of what he knew. The accurate description of Balam, the woman in the playground, the sight of his sister… it all added up to a compelling argument for making a leap of faith.

He retrieved the card and fiddled with it between his fingers, intrigued by Derek Lansdale's title. Was this guy really in charge of a parapsychology department at a university? And did he really have a Ph.D.?

I mean, a Ph.D.? In *that*?

Ridiculous.

He closed his eyes and finally drifted off into a vivid dream. Cassy stood in front of him, but not in a sinister, captive way; the scene felt pleasant. Sun shone down upon them, red leaves grew on trees, and the greenest of grass surrounded the path. It was a memory. He was teaching her to ride the bike. The same bike that she was riding when she was hit by…

No. This is a nice memory. He banished such horrible thoughts and enjoyed his happy dream; he didn't get many.

She was riding without the stabilisers for the first time. His parents were somewhere arguing, but it didn't matter, he was there to enjoy this pivotal moment. He was sharing this experience with her.

The bike wobbled, stumbling from side to side. Eddie's eleven-year-old self ran up to her and caught the bike before she could fall off, but as a result, it meant the bike and Cassy fell on top of him. She found it hilarious. He didn't at first, but he laughed along eventually.

Then she turned to him and smiled.

"I'm sorry for falling on you," she giggled.

"It's okay," Eddie beamed, brushing himself off and helping her to her feet.

"Are you going to save me?"

Eddie turned his head with a start. This wasn't part of the memory.

"What?"

"Are you going to save me, Eddie?"

Her eyes turned to bright lights and her mouth unbolted into a mind-numbing shriek.

CRACK.

Eddie woke up with a start, drenched in sweat and panting. He sat up, expecting someone to be there with him, but unsure why.

There wasn't anything. He was alone. The room was as it was when he went to bed. He was on the sofa bed, the living room was empty, and the trees stood still through the gap in the curtains.

To the side of him was his glass of water. The rim had cracked and some water had leaked as a result, but it still stood motionless on the table beside him.

Then it cracked again.

SMASH!

The glass exploded into hundreds of shattered pieces that fired around the room. Eddie shielded himself, but it was too late; tiny fragments of glass were in his hair and stuck to his bare torso. He dabbed his face and felt a cut, blood trickling down his chin.

"Shit."

He stood and brushed his shorts, legs, and chest off. He took his towel off the back of the armchair and brushed the glass from his face before dabbing his cut.

Shuffle.

He turned his head. The sound had come from behind him. He could see no movement in the shadows, no evidence that this sound had come from anywhere but his mind.

He flicked the light switch, but the lights did not come on.

It meant nothing. It was just a fuse switch that needed to be flicked back on.

He remained in darkness and continued to brush glass off his face.

Crunch.

He shot his head around again.

Dumping the towel on the floor, he edged his way toward a dark corner across the room — the dark corner where he was sure the sound had come from.

"Is anyone there?"

He wasn't sure why he asked this, as he really didn't want anyone to answer. Luckily for him, no one did.

Shuffle. Crunch.

The noises came again, from the exact spot he was staring at. It was pure black; he couldn't be sure there was nothing there. But there couldn't be. There couldn't.

"Is anyone there?"

Silence ensued. Then it was broken.

"*Eddie*," came a whisper.

He couldn't tell who it was; the whisper was too faint for him to be able to decipher any of its characteristics.

"Jenny? Lacy? Is that you?"

"*Eddie...*" came the whisper again, this time a little louder, though still relatively soft. It was a voice in distress.

"Who's there?" he asked, edging closer to the darkness, just a few steps away.

"*Eddie...*" it repeated. It was a girl's voice.

He reached the shadow. Stood in front of it. His toe crossed the threshold of the darkness.\

"*Eddie... it's Cassy...*"

He froze. Stumped. Rooted to the floor.

Cassy?

Before he could conceive what was happening, he was launched off his feet and across the room, landing on his back. He tried to get up, but couldn't; whatever it was, it was pushing him to the floor with more strength than he could fight.

"Cassy? Is that you?" he struggled.

It cackled.

This wasn't Cassy.

It was *her*.

He closed his eyes, tried to turn away, tried to refuse the sight — but she held his focus with an adamant, grave determination.

The hollow black eyes, the empty mouth, the grey skin, the black greasy hair...

She was all there.

The beast.

The servant of Balam.

Balam, who had his sister.

"What do you want, you bitch?"

Mistake.

He was lifted higher into the air. A tight fist wrapped around his neck. He couldn't make out the form through the darkness and the dizziness of his vision, but he could feel its cold, clammy hand pressing against his throat.

His feet dangled helplessly. He could see the faint outline of a figure and thrashed out and fought against it, but his hands just went through it. Like it wasn't there.

But it was.

A pain flashed across his arm as he was lunged across the room and left to slam into another wall.

He collapsed onto his knees, clutching his bicep, feeling something — a scrape, or a cut.

The light switched on and Jenny appeared in the doorway.

"Eddie? What the hell?"

Eddie couldn't reply. All he could do was dab the bleeding wound on his arm.

"What have you done?" Jenny asked.

"You can see it too?" he answered.

This thing had created this wound.

And she could see it.

Dammit, she can see it...

That meant he couldn't fight it anymore.

This wasn't in his head.

She could see it. He could feel it. What had happened was real.

He needed help.

CHAPTER NINETEEN

"*S*o you want to bring some weirdo paranormal nut into my house and have them watch you sleep?" Jenny said, her hands on her hips.

Lacy sat back in her chair and smirked, finding the whole thing amusing. Eddie glanced at her, sitting forward on his sofa bed and running his hands through his hair.

"I think it would really help me, Jenny," he said. "Something's going on with me, and maybe they would help me figure it out."

"Yes, Eddie, something is going on with you, and it is not paranormal — it's pretty fucking abnormal, but it's not ghosts."

"Lacy?" Eddie looked to the voice of reason for help. "Are you okay with this?"

"Hey, don't ask me, ask the boss," she retorted, refusing to get involved.

"I'm not having it." Jenny shook her head as she straightened up coasters and shuffled magazines into a neat pile.

"Jenny, come on, they aren't even going to bother you," Eddie pleaded. "They are coming to study me, see what I do. They won't even be going upstairs."

"But you're still going to have some crazy people in my house."

"Jenny, please. They say this is the only way."

Jenny sighed, leant against the armchair, and placed her fingers on her sinus. She couldn't believe this was even a conversation she was having. He was her oldest friend, but he needed rational help rather than a bunch of ghost-freaks.

Although, he had been there for her in times when she'd needed a leap of faith. She had spent many nights crying into his arms after revealing her sexuality to her parents; not once did he falter or question her choices.

"How are they going to help you?" she asked, and Eddie perked up as if sensing he may have a chance.

"They think there is something hanging around me, and they say it may be why I keep sleepwalking and waking up on the lawn. They think if they saw me sleep, when I'm at my most vulnerable, they may be able to get some idea why it is these things keep happening to me."

Jenny groaned. "I still think it's total bullshit. If you've got problems, it's because of you, not because of Casper." She sighed and shrugged her shoulders. "But if you really think it's going to help you, then… fine. Whatever."

Eddie jumped up and gave Jenny a big bear-hug.

"Thank you, Jenny, you're the best. I love you!"

"Yeah, yeah."

"So when are they coming?"

"Tonight?"

She turned to Lacy. "Fancy a night out then?"

"What? Screw that!" Lacy said. "I want to see what these weirdos are going to do to him."

Eddie snorted. Being honest, he barely believed he was going through with this himself. But he couldn't take another vicar or psychic jumping away from him and recoiling in horror. Even if this was bullshit, at least it was another option he could eliminate.

But Eddie could never have been prepared for the events of that night.

CHAPTER TWENTY

The paranormal investigators weren't at all what Eddie was expecting. Saying that, he wasn't entirely sure what he was expecting; but these two, professional-looking, educated men were not it.

Derek introduced himself first. A tall man, wearing a waist-coat over a smart white shirt, a black tie, and black trousers. He had neatly parted hair, a tidy goatee, and large, circular, black glasses. He presented himself as a thorough professional, greeting Eddie, then Jenny and Lacy, with a firm shake of the hand and a welcome smile.

Levi followed Derek in, carrying a bag over his shoulder and two overflowing suit-cases full of equipment in either hand. He dumped them in the living room and gave Eddie a limp handshake. He was introduced by Derek as his "best student," prompting Levi to look a little smug as he brushed his messy hair out of his face. He too was wearing a shirt, tie, and trousers, but his top button was undone, his shirt untucked, and his trousers were baggy.

"Your best student?" Eddie enquired.

"Yes, my very best," Derek said, walking past Eddie and examining all corners of the living room.

"He's my mentor in my degree," Levi interjected. "I'm currently doing my thesis on sleep paralysis induced by paranormal phenomena."

"So you work at a university?" Lacy asked Derek, bemused, who nodded in return.

Eddie didn't need to glance at Jenny in the armchair behind him to know what face she was pulling. He could imagine her turning her head away and rolling her eyes. He could, however, see Lacy perched on the arm of the sofa with a smile, both intrigued and fascinated.

"So, Eddie, could you take us to your bedroom?" Derek prompted.

"You're standing in it." Eddie chuckled at the awkwardness of the situation. "This is my sofa bed."

"Ah, I see."

Lacy jumped off the sofa bed to allow Derek a closer look. He inspected and scrutinised each crevice and fold of the sofa, not making it at all clear what he was looking for. As he searched, he continued to ask Eddie questions.

"So, this woman, you say you've seen her before?"

"Yeah, I was knocked out and put in a coma as a child, I saw her then. Then I almost drowned and was put in a coma a few months ago; I saw her again then. I say *coma*... I was technically braindead. Then, in my therapist's office the other day..."

"You were braindead?"

"Yes, they said only one in a billion wake up after being declared braindead."

"Far less than that actually."

"There's also, I mean, as well as this woman there was..." He trailed off. He'd only spoken about this woman to Jenny, and hadn't mentioned Balam yet. Saying he believed a three-headed demon may have his sister's soul was probably more than she would be able to take.

Derek straightened up and rubbed his chin. "I see. And how long were you in a coma, each time?"

"When I was a kid it was, like, a few days. I think the last one was a few months."

Derek nodded and strode past him to Levi. "I want one here, here, and here," he instructed, pointing at various corners of the room. "Set the EVP microphone by the bed, set the ultraviolet camera here…"

"The ultraviolet camera?" Eddie was curious, and a little freaked out.

"Yes, it takes a picture should anything, 'spooky,' shall we say, presents itself." He gestured at Levi to set the camera up facing the sofa bed. "Then, Eddie, I think we should allow you to go to sleep."

After half an hour, everything was set up. Jenny and Lacy were in their bed, Derek and Levi were in the kitchen staring at various monitors, and Eddie was laying on the sofa bed gazing at the ceiling. He glanced at the clock that read 11.32 p.m., with no idea how he was going get to sleep with various cameras pointing at him. Yet, after a matter of minutes, he found himself lightly drifting off. His eyes grew heavy, he floated off to sleep.

Relaxation consumed him, every muscle in his body soft, sinking into a dreamless sleep… A dreamless sleep that became a sleep of pleasant dreams… A sleep of pleasant dreams that turned into nightmares…

And there she was again; her body floating above him, sucking every piece of his life out of his mouth.

He woke up shrieking.

He screamed and screamed and screamed until he regained his senses. The first thing he saw was the clock. 2.45 a.m. The next thing he acknowledged was the ultraviolet camera flashing recurrently, bright-white lights blinding him every half a second.

He leant forward to grab at it but it fell on the floor. Once he was no longer in the camera's view, it ceased flashing.

He raised his head and gawped at the state the room. The armchair was overturned, light bulbs in the lights were smashed, curtains were torn down, and papers were ripped all over the floor. Everyone was there. And they were all staring at Eddie with terrified, bloodshot eyes.

Levi huddled in the corner of the room, panting heavily, shielding his body with his arms. Lacy and Jenny were embracing each other, huddling against the wall.

Derek was on his knees in the middle of the room. His hair was messy, swept back aerodynamically, as if he had been caught in the middle of a huge gale. His once neat suit was now scruffy and dishevelled. He held an arm out to Eddie cautiously, keeping his distance.

"Eddie? Is that you?"

"Yes," Eddie snapped. "Who else would it be?"

"Right, Eddie, we are going to need you to stay as still as you can."

"Why? What's happened?"

Everyone's jaw was dropped. They couldn't take their eyes off of him. They all kept a safe distance, scared yet fascinated. Eventually, Jenny stepped forward.

"Do you really have no idea?"

CHAPTER TWENTY-ONE

*E*ddie sat at the table opposite Derek and Levi, each of them fidgeting their fingers around a mug of coffee they barely drank. Jenny and Lacy stood in the doorway with their arms around each other, wanting to be there, but not willing to get too close.

"Eddie, what I'm about to tell you," Derek began, fumbling to find the right words, "is hard to take, at first. But I believe it. I believe it one hundred percent, with every bone in my body. In fact, we've been waiting for something like this to come along for quite a while."

"Okay…" Eddie looked weakly from Derek to Levi, an odd sense of despair overcoming him. People rarely prepared you like this for news if it was good. What made it worse was that, despite his trepidation, Derek looked giddy at the idea there may be something wrong.

"Your dream, when you were in the coma both as a child and the more recent incident," Derek began, then paused, glancing at his coffee and taking in a big, deep breath. "It wasn't a coma. There's a reason you were braindead…"

Derek stopped fumbling his hands around the mug, and

made his upmost effort to stay still and direct his full focus on Eddie.

"When you were braindead, it's because... well, you actually died."

Eddie narrowed his eye and sat back, looking at him oddly. "But I can't have died. I mean, I'm alive now."

"Yes, you are alive, I'm not doubting it. What I'm saying is that, for however long you were in the coma for, that wasn't a coma. You were actually brain-dead, were you not? You, however temporarily, crossed over to, well, I don't know quite how to put this... the other side."

"The other side? As in, like, *beyond*?"

"Exactly! What happened, is, well — when you crossed over to the other side, you came in contact with something from... the other world. A world where you don't belong, Eddie, as you are part of the living. But I also believe there is a reason it latched onto you specifically, and why it is that you were able to cross into this other world whilst still alive, something I have never known anyone else to be able to do."

"So I was in heaven?"

"Oh, Lord, no."

Eddie looked around, on edge.

"Maybe ever so briefly, but... my boy, you were in Hell. In a demon world. A world that belongs only to evil, along with the worst souls that have ever lived, suffering their eternal fate, and the devil himself."

He froze.

"Eddie, we believe that you are paranormally vulnerable."

"Paranormally vulnerable?"

"You have a gift, Eddie. A remarkable gift only one in a million, to a hundred million people have. You have what we call — the sight. It means you have the ability to see things, feel things, that the rest of us cannot."

Jenny scoffed and turned her face away. "This is bullshit,"

she muttered to herself, but loud enough for everyone else to hear.

"So when you crossed over to this demon world," Derek continued, ignoring Jenny and focusing on Eddie, who was listening attentively. "This thing, this entity — it saw that it could latch on to you, and that's what it did."

"So this thing has, what, stuck itself to me?"

"That would be a good way to put it. You see, when you crossed over the first time, it was only for a few days. It didn't have nearly enough time to fully attach itself to you. But when you crossed over the second time, it was for months. You actually died, and, well… it had enough time. It had enough time to see you were paranormally gifted, stick its nasty arms around you, hold tight and never let go. And now it's left the beyond. You have brought it back to our world. And it doesn't intend to leave."

Eddie sat back in his chair and rubbed his eyes. It was 4:00 a.m., far before his normal morning wake-up time, and he was tired. This was a lot to take in. He truly did not know what to make of it. It would all make a lovely explanation, but rational thought would lead to him to believe he simply had mental health issues. Psychosis, maybe? Schizophrenia? Not that he was some sort of gifted ghost-person, crossing over to the other side.

"There's more," Eddie admitted. He hadn't told anyone about what else he'd seen when he was there, but maybe these guys could offer him some explanation, some hope.

They raised their eyebrows expectantly, yet with an air of patience.

"There was more than just this demon woman entity thing. There was something else. It said its name was Balam."

Derek exchanged a cold look with Levi, as if sharing an unspoken concern.

"Are you sure?"

"Yes, but there's more… this entity said it was Balam's slave."

"Who is Balam?" interjected Lacy.

"Balam," Derek answered, "is one of the princes of hell. One of the devil's generals, who commands legions of demons. This entity that has attached itself to you will be but a mere slave to Balam – you see, if it is in fact Balam, that is what you are up against. He has three heads–"

"One of a human, a bull, and a ram," Eddie finished, nodding. "I know. I saw him."

"You mean," Levi's eyes become wide with anticipation, "you actually saw Balam?"

"And he had my sister. My dead sister. He had her and he tormented me with her."

Jenny exhaled, clearly exasperated, fidgeting uncomfortably. Lacy put her hand on her arm in an attempt to calm her, but even she could feel that Jenny was about to blow.

Derek and Levi leant back and exchanged looks. Derek rubbed his beard, loosened his tie, and undid the top button of his shirt; the first sign of willing untidiness he had let himself show in all of the commotion.

He leant forward and looked Eddie directly in the eyes.

"Listen, Eddie, because this is of the utmost importance. We can help drive out this entity. We can help detach it from you. I can't guarantee anything, but we can certainly try. But as for Balam… for what you saw of your sister…" He glanced at Levi, whose face said the same thing. "Well, I imagine if you saw her, it was her soul. And if Balam has her soul, there is little we could do to come up against such a demon as that."

"But I thought you were a university scholar? How can you be a demonologist who's scared of demons?"

"A lion tamer will still leave an untamed lion alone, Eddie. We can help with this entity, the slave of Balam, but as for Balam himself… I'm sorry."

Eddie looked away. He felt a tear form in the corner of his eye and he used all the force he had in his body to quell it. He longed for his sister. He longed for that empty void, and he was used to that; but to leave his sister being tormented in Hell was not an option.

Then he tried to remember that he didn't believe in this stuff. Tried to convince himself it wasn't real.

But he had seen it.

It's just made-up games. The boogeyman is a child's nightmare, he assured himself. They were empty thoughts made from empty words — just manifestations of an angry, confused young man.

"One thing I will say, is that you are gifted, Eddie. To have been able to go into the demon world, not once, but twice, and return... it is something no man has ever done. If we can face this entity, maybe I could help you."

"How?"

"I could help you to harness your gift. Teach you how to use it. Then we can see the extent of what this ability can reach. I mean, if we can control your ability to flicker into that world, imagine-" He curtailed his words, getting ahead of himself.

"Is that a promise?"

Derek looked down. His thoughts grounded himself, reigning his ambition back in.

"First, we face a mighty challenge, Eddie. A challenge with this entity that has taken you over. That's new ground for us, also."

They shared a few moments of uncomfortable reflection.

"So, what now?"

"Well, that's where it becomes difficult." Derek took a long pause, gathering his thoughts, deciding on the best way to articulate what he needed to say. "This thing, this — 'entity' — it does not belong in this world. It belongs in the other. And its mere presence here is unnatural, an abomination. Both you, and it, should technically be dead. And this thing has far less right to be here than you do. So it's going to try and take it from you."

"It's going to take what from me?"

"Neither of you can coexist in this world, I'm afraid. It's stuck itself to you and it wants to take your place. So it's going to make you weaker, and weaker, and weaker, until it takes the life you have gained back from fate, allowing it your place on this plane of existence."

It wanted to take his life? *Jesus,* he thought. *It can have it.*

"So what can I do?" Eddie asked helplessly.

Derek said nothing. He stood, put his hands in his pockets, and thought carefully. He seemed to be struggling to provide the answer.

Eddie looked to Levi, who was looking at Derek for answers just as much as Eddie was.

"So, what, there's nothing I can do? This thing's just going to latch onto me and take me?"

Derek sighed. "The only thing I could suggest, is…" He pursed his lips and looked around uncomfortably. "An exorcism."

"An exorcism?"

"Yes. And we will perform it, in return for your permission to fully document it for our university research."

Jenny stood forward. "That's it, I've had enough. I think it's time you go."

Eddie scowled at her. "Jenny!"

"No, I've had enough. I've entertained this loony idea, I did what you asked — now it's time that we, I don't know, perhaps bring some reality to the situation. It's far more likely that you are all nuts."

"Jenny–" Lacy stepped forward to put an arm around her, but Jenny nudged her way out of it.

"No, sorry, but no. It's been very nice you being here, and I hope you enjoyed your coffee, but now it's time to go. It's time to pack up your equipment and crawl back to the university that is far happier entertaining your ridiculous theories than we are."

Sighing, Derek and Levi rose and began solemnly packing away their equipment.

Eddie turned to Jenny. "What the hell is wrong with you?"

"What's wrong with me?" She had her hands on her hips, ready for an argument. "What's wrong with *you*? You need mental help, Eddie, that's what it is — and so do they, being honest. I will help you to get your help. I will drive you to therapy. But one thing I will not do is entertain a freak show in my own house. If you want that, you can get your own."

Jenny stormed out the room, slammed the door, and Lacy chased after her. Eddie heard her feet stomping up the stairs and her bedroom door slamming above him. This was followed by the sound of the front door opening and closing.

Eddie darted to the hallway, hoping to catch Derek and Levi before they left, but it was too late. They were gone.

And he was stood there, alone.

MILLENNIUM NIGHT

CHAPTER TWENTY-TWO

*E*ddie steps onto the porch, willing his heavy breathing to subside. He leans against the door frame, rubs his hand over his head and through his hair. He feels inside his pocket for a cigarette, withdraws it, then puts it in his mouth and lights it.

Beatrice, the girl's mother, appears beside him.

"Do you mind?" he asks, indicating his cigarette.

"Not so long as you give me one," she replies, and Eddie obliges. She looks to have aged even more within the last few hours. The bags under her eyes are heavier and the definition of her wrinkles all the more apparent when reflected in the moonlight. Her hair is grey and tatty, almost knotted into a mound. Seeing as she has a sixteen-year-old daughter, Eddie decides she can't be as old as she looks.

I suppose this kind of ordeal ages you.

"I can't thank you enough for coming to help her," she says quietly.

"Thank me when it's over," Eddie says. Although he doesn't admit it to her, or even to himself, this is the first time in almost five years that he feels completely overwhelmed. He is losing, and he knows it.

"Well, whether you help her or not, you believed me. That's more than anyone else has done."

"Ah well, in this day and age, people like to put it down to various mental health diagnoses. And in most cases, you know, they would of course be right."

He takes a deep, inward drag of his cigarette and closes his eyes. He doesn't normally smoke anymore, not regularly anyway; but he always has a packet stashed away for this type of occasion. He needs it. Especially now, as this demon is one tough son of a bitch.

A huge clash resounds throughout the house. Eddie immediately turns his head. After prematurely stubbing his cigarette out, he gallops up the stairs and bursts into the bedroom.

It is calm. Uncomfortably calm. The demon-infested girl lays on the bed, breathing heavily and with a croak on each inward inhale. It gazes at Eddie with a smile.

Eddie watches it. He tries to decide what to make of this new-found lethargy. He knows the demon is playing him, retaining control, mocking him. Still, it takes him by surprise, and he isn't sure what to do with it.

"You seem calm," he observes, then tells himself he's an idiot.

'You seem calm?' What the hell is that meant to do?

"I was just waiting for you, Eddie ma boy," comes an unnaturally manly voice for the face of a young girl. It is a unique voice, one that stands apart from the earlier voice coming from the demon.

"Your voice has changed. Am I still talking to Balam?"

"The one and only."

Eddie leans against a dresser. The drawers from the unit rest in pieces all over the room, as do the previous contents of the draws; but the dresser itself stands in place, balanced precariously without the weight holding it down. Eddie uses it to support his tired legs.

"And where did you come from, may I ask?"

"Why do you need to know?"

"As I would like to know where I am sending you back to."

Its grin spreads. The demon sits up, opens its mouth, and lets out a scream that forces Eddie against the back wall, along with various items that rise from the floor.

It reaches out an arm and slashes it like a claw. Even though they are across the room from one another, the slash still causes Eddie to fall to his knees. He closes his eyes and winces in pain, feeling his chest, blood soaking through his shirt.

"That hurt you?" the demon boasts.

Eddie lifts up his shirt, revealing three fresh wounds over his scarred chest.

"You aren't the first demon to try to intimidate me."

"Intimidate you? Maybe I should remind you what I did to your sister."

"Shut up."

"She was naked when you saw her last, right? Did you see the scars?"

"*Quiet!*" Eddie throws the holy water at it, smashing the bottle against the wall beside its head. At first it howls in pain, then in masochistic pleasure.

"I raped her. I tortured her. And I ate bits and pieces of her whilst she begged on her knees for me to stop."

Eddie wipes his eyes.

"I am going to fucking destroy you."

1995

CHAPTER TWENTY-THREE

*E*ddie sat in the waiting room twiddling his thumbs. Doctors' waiting rooms were always so depressing. The pattern of the wallpaper was the style he'd expect from a grandmother's curtains. The toys left to keep children occupied were usually just wooden blocks dispersed around the floor and the magazines were usually women's magazines dated from around three months prior.

He glanced at the two other people occupying the waiting room. To his left was an old man who kept his walking stick propped up in front of him, resting both hands upon it. He coughed every few seconds; not just a gentle, normal cough, but a dramatic cough that sounded as if he was bringing up a dead cat. He wore a flat cap that had more stains on it than Eddie could place.

To his right was a younger lady, heavily pregnant, with vacant eyes. She stared gormlessly at the bottom corner of the room, with bags under her eyes and her hair a scraggy mess. He could see all the veins in her arms.

Eddie mentally urged the doctor to hurry up, peering down the corridor, hoping to be called in as soon as possible. He felt awkward and out of place. He usually felt awkward in any social situation, but sitting between an old man coughing up his lungs and a doped-up mother-to-be was even worse.

Finally, the doctor came into the waiting room and called his name. He stood slowly, supporting himself against the wall, trying not to fall on his shaking legs. Using the walls and the chairs to keep himself propped up, he made his way into the corridor. He took a moment to rest, catching his breath, allowing the blurs to fade from his eyesight and his dizziness to subside. He used the wall to guide his way into the doctor's room and delicately sat on the chair opposite him.

The doctor was a middle-aged man with a bald patch. He wore the a white coat over a shirt and tie. He sat toward Eddie with a large smile, making Eddie feel at ease.

"Eddie," the doctor said, glancing at his notes to make sure of his name. "How are you today?"

"I'm okay," Eddie croaked, forcing the words through his sore throat.

"And what can I help you with?"

Eddie took a deep, wheezing inhale of breath. He was still recovering from the walk from the waiting room.

"I – I seem to be becoming weaker."

The doctor sat back and chewed his pen.

"How so?"

"Two weeks ago I was fine," Eddie explained. "But now I'm out of breath walking down the corridor, my throat is always dry, and I feel dizzy when I walk. I can't explain it, but I feel like I'm fifty years older."

"Okay. I'm going to take your pulse, is that all right?"

Eddie nodded and the doctor took out his stethoscope. He lifted Eddie's shirt to reveal a body far thinner than Eddie was used to. His arms were bony and his skin was tight against his ribs.

The Doctor placed the end of the stethoscope over Eddie's

heart and listened carefully. He took it away and thought for a few moments.

"I'm going to take your blood pressure as well, is that all right?"

Eddie nodded again. The doctor took out a pad and fastened it around Eddie's bare arm, clasping it together through its Velcro strap. Eddie felt it squeeze against his bicep. After a few moments it retracted, and the doctor looked at the results.

"Yes, Eddie, okay," he said. "I am slightly worried. Your heart rate is lower than I'd expect and your blood pressure is too. Have there been any changes to your circumstances, Eddie? Any drugs, new sexual partners, anything?"

"No."

"I need you to be honest with me, Eddie."

"I am, Doctor."

The doctor nodded then typed on his computer's keyboard.

"I'm going to make you an appointment at the hospital, Eddie, so one of my colleagues can give you a more thorough examination, involving x-rays, and so on. We can do it in about a week's time. Is there any particular day or time that would suit you?"

"Whenever."

"Okay," the doctor said, and booked Eddie an appointment.

* * *

EDDIE TRUDGED HOME, taking it step by agonising step. People barged past and almost knocked him to the ground a few times. Despite the warm sun he felt cold, so he wrapped his jacket around himself.

He paused for a moment, leaning against the wall to gather his energy, feeling desperately weak. He was only half way home; he wasn't going to make it without a more substantial recuperation time. Spotting a café a few shops up, he used the wall to support himself as he limped his way to the entrance and shuffled in.

He contemplated the menu displayed above the counter. He didn't know why he bothered, coffee shop drink options were always the same: latte, cappuccino, mocha or Americano. He requested an Americano and leant against the counter as he waited. He bowed his head and found his eyes beginning to close. One moment he was gazing upon the cheesecake behind the counter, the next minute the back of his eyelids were all he saw and he felt his muscles relax. Just before he fell from the counter, he became alert again to the sound of his Americano being ready.

A few metres away, a baby's eyes fixated on him whilst having an uncontrollable crying fit, crying and crying and crying, not once averting its glare from Eddie.

Eddie glanced around, unsure what to do.

The mother rushed her baby out. As soon as the baby crossed the doorway into the street, the crying ceased and the baby seemed to find peace.

Eddie frowned, feeling slightly perturbed.

He took a seat next to the window, sipped his drink, and peered around the café. It was a nice place, with classical furniture and quotes from various books on the walls. Being late in the afternoon, he expected it wasn't the most popular time, which was why there was only a couple across the room and an old man and his dog behind him.

He gazed out of the window at the people passing by. Everyone was always in such a hurry. He saw a few businessmen in suits, talking carelessly to their business partners scurrying beside them. He noticed a jogger on the other side of the road, earphones from their Walkman keeping the world tuned out, drifting happily along in their vest and shorts.

An elderly couple crossed the road and a man got out of his

car to help them. Eddie smiled. There was good in this world after all.

That's when he saw her.

She stared at him from across the street. Inside the window of a furniture shop, the ominous figure lurched. Its outlines were unclear behind the reflections in the window, but the sick feeling in the pit of his stomach gave Eddie no doubt that she was there.

"You're not real," he whispered.

It didn't move. It didn't even draw breath. Its scraggly, greasy hair fell in mounds over its face. Its skin was grey and cracked, wounds bled on its arms, and its pupils were completely black. Despite not being able to see it clearly, he could see its eyes.

Those were the eyes that made every part of his body shake.

"You are not real," he spoke again, causing the couple across the room to glance at him before returning to their flirtations.

Eddie dropped his head and shut his eyes. He scrunched his eyelids closed, pressing hard, refusing to acknowledge it. He shook his head, squeezing his eyelids together until they hurt.

He lifted his head and opened his eyes. The woman was gone.

He smiled. He was right. It was all part of his subconscious. A figment of his imagination. Like Jenny had said, he just needed mental health help. Nothing more.

Nothing paranormal about it, just a trick of a weakened mind.

Just as he began to relax, something threw him from his seat.

He slid across the surface and crashed into a table.

His hands clutched at his scalp and he writhed in pain. His head had been hit hard and it hurt. He withdrew his fingers and looked at the blood on his hands.

Everyone else in the coffee shop was looking at him,

assuming that, through his stupidity, he had somehow fallen off his chair.

He leant up, his eyes darting around the room, scanning the menacingly innocent faces staring at him. He must have just fallen off his chair. The only explanation. He didn't know how he'd done it. But he was growing weaker; maybe he had just slid off, or there had been a problem with the chair.

He assured himself there was a rational explanation.

He rose to his feet, brushing himself off, uncomfortably smiling at those around him who stared. No one asked if he was okay, they just acted as obstinate voyeurs.

Without any warning, Eddie was taken off his feet again. This time he was pushed through the air and across the room, slammed against the wall and held there, pressed up against a framed quote, then let go so he could fall flat on his face.

Everyone in the coffee shop was off their seat, straddling the wall furthest away from Eddie. They were agape, aghast, protecting themselves; no thought of helping whatsoever.

Eddie just lay there. Staying down. Maybe if he stayed on the floor, he wouldn't be flung anywhere, and it couldn't get to him. His head pounded and every bone in his back ached.

A heaviness on his legs pushed them down. Something was on them. His neck stiffened and he couldn't turn it. The feebleness of his bones and his muscles became all the more apparent under the invisible strain.

He knew what it was. He knew what it was doing. But he could do nothing to stop the *snap* that resounded around the coffee shop.

No matter how hard he tried, he could not explain that one.

CHAPTER TWENTY-FOUR

*E*ddie sat in still silence. Lacy aimed a smile at him as she drove, attempting to reassure him.

"So what happened?" she asked.

"I... I don't even know," Eddie admitted. In his mind he was torn, struggling to make sense of it all.

Shooting pains continued to race up and down his leg. He rubbed them, attempted to soothe the agony. He hadn't been able to put any pressure on his feet since he had been flung into a wall, but he felt too scared to say anything. He did not wish to face the judgmental stares Jenny would give him after Lacy had regaled his story.

So what the hell had happened?

He knew he had been lifted from the floor, into the air and across the room. There were witnesses to it, surely. Not particularly helpful witnesses; witnesses who likely doubted their eyes. Witnesses who were probably in as much denial as Eddie, but witnesses nonetheless.

Then how come no one said anything about it? Had they seen what Eddie thought they had seen? Or had they been freaked out because he did it to himself?

These were traits typical of psychosis. Eddie knew a little about it, having had doctors talk to him shortly after Cassy had died regarding a potential diagnosis, before instead diagnosing him with post-traumatic stress disorder. People with psychosis saw and experienced things that were completely true in their eyes, and harboured stubborn beliefs that their disillusionment was true. Maybe that's what was happening to Eddie.

In that case, how was he so aware of it? If he had flung himself across the room to feign some kind of attack, then surely he wouldn't be able to recognise that possibility if he was so deep in his disillusionment? From what he had read, people with deep psychosis were not aware that the reality they perceived was potentially not reality.

Maybe he just needed help. Maybe Jenny was right.

"Where is Jenny?" Eddie asked, noticing that Lacy picking him up on her own.

"Oh, you know Jenny," Lacy answered, doing her best to avoid the subject. "She's… Jenny."

"She hates me, doesn't she? She thinks I'm desperate for attention."

Lacy sighed. She couldn't argue with him; he was right. Jenny had ranted and raved every night before bed for the past few weeks, going on and on and on and on. Lacy knew she was a more relaxed person than Jenny — that was why they worked so well; they complimented each other. But even Lacy was starting to become frustrated over the constant threats to throw her lifelong best friend out onto the street.

"He's full of shit," she would go on, using a similar pattern of words and meanings each time. "He won't get proper help. Instead, he puts it all to some hocus pocus crap."

Lacy would put her hand on Jenny's back and tell her it was okay, everything would work out. She would hug her and kiss her neck and try to distract her the best way she knew how, but eventually she would give up. If Jenny's mind wasn't in it, Lacy didn't want to have sex. If Jenny would rather go on about Eddie, if that's really where her thoughts lay, Lacy would go without. She wasn't interested in being with a body without a mind.

They pulled up outside the house and Lacy made her way to Eddie's door to help him out. Eddie may be disillusioned, but he was obviously extremely ill. His feebleness was not a lie and Lacy was getting worried. He was constantly pale and struggling to walk more than a few steps without his muscles giving out. He reminded Lacy of how her grandma was just before she died.

"What did the doctor say?"

"He's made me an appointment with the hospital. He's concerned."

Lacy nodded, unsure what else she could say. What comfort can you give to someone who's seriously ill? 'At least you still have a roof over your head' wouldn't cut it, seeing as Eddie barely had that.

Once inside, Lacy helped Eddie to the sofa bed and he lay down. He closed his eyes as Lacy went to the kitchen to fetch him a glass of water. He was so out of breath, despite a small walk from the car to the house.

As Lacy returned with a glass of water, Jenny burst down the stairs and into the room.

"Hey baby, are you-" She stopped when she saw Lacy handing Eddie a glass of water. She glared at him, pursing her lips together and folding her arms.

"Please, Jenny, don't start," Lacy said, seeing that look in her eyes.

"How was the doctor?" Jenny asked.

"Eddie said his doctor is concerned."

"He can answer for himself."

"Enough, Jenny." Lacy rushed up to her, putting her hands

on her arms, rubbing them and smiling at her. "Whatever you think, he is really, really ill, and he needs our help."

"Guys, I don't feel so good..." Eddie mumbled. His body was furiously shaking, his lip quivering, and his hands were aimlessly clawing at the side of the sofa.

Lacy ran over to him, followed by Jenny, putting her hands on his shoulder. She placed a hand on his forehead to check his temperature.

"He's burning up," she told Jenny, who placed her hand on his forehead too and felt how hot he was. The anger she had directed at Eddie turned to worry as his shaking turned to a seizure.

"Phone an ambulance," Lacy instructed.

Eddie's eyes went blank and his whole body convulsed. Lacy stayed with him, her hands pressed over his, as Jenny rushed for the phone. The sound of Jenny talking to the 9-9-9 operator faded into the distance as his mouth filled with foam.

Eddie could tell he was having a seizure. He could feel his muscles shaking but was helpless to stop it. In his eye line he saw a black dot growing bigger. Then he saw her.

She stood over him, smiling, lurking. Lacy was to his side, reassuring, completely unaware. Still, this woman remained.

The last thing he saw before he blacked out was her open mouth with black and bile dripping down her chin. She leapt toward Eddie and into his chest. His chest rose into the air as his seizure grew fierce.

Then it went black.

He came around in flashes.

Flash one: a man in a green outfit sat over him, reassuring him it was going to be okay. Jenny and Lacy held each other on the far side of the room. He could see Jenny was crying.

Black.

Flash two: he could hear an engine running and sirens wailing. He shook from side to side and felt them turn a corner.

"Please…" he began to speak.

Black.

Flash three: he saw tiles and lights above him pass quickly, all following the same pattern. He saw the underside of a chin, then saw the white coat the owner of the chin was wearing.

"Please don't let me go into a coma…"

"Okay, Eddie, it's going to be okay."

"She'll come back… don't let her come back…"

"Relax, please. Where is that damn sedative?"

Black.

Flash four: a lamp light shone on him. There was commotion all around the room. People in white lab coats and blue scrubs rushed.

"If you let me go braindead she'll take me…"

"Why is he awake? I thought he was under!"

"She'll take me…"

"Why the Christ is he awake? Sort it out!"

Black.

Flash five: Jenny sat over him, clutching his hand. He could feel the tightness of her warm grasp around his fingers.

"Don't let her take me…"

Black.

CHAPTER TWENTY-FIVE

*E*ddie sat up in his bed, his leg propped up in a cast, his hand dabbing his fork at the miserable hospital food. Jenny sat beside him, laughing at how disgusting it was, reassuring Eddie that she would pop to the local and get something substantial as soon as the doctor arrived.

"Thank God," Eddie responded. "As if I'm not bad enough already, it's like they are trying to kill me."

Jenny chuckled and rubbed his arm affectionately. Eddie smiled at her. He felt like he had his best friend back. Despite the whole ordeal he had gone through, he had her back.

He recalled his dreams from the previous night. He'd had two and, although he didn't often remember his dreams, he recalled them vividly. The first was about him and Jenny opening up a pencil shop in America. He had no idea where this had come from; neither he nor Jenny had expressed a desire to live in America, start a business, or had any kind of inclination whatsoever toward pencils.

The second had been slightly uncomfortable. He had been trapped in a jar of mayonnaise. Eddie knew there was far more to it than that, but that was all that he could recall.

Either way, he was extremely grateful he had not slipped into another coma or become braindead again. The last time he had been stuck in a hospital bed, he had found himself haunted with images that had plagued his conscious thoughts ever since — but not this time. He had not 'crossed over' as the paranormal experts had bizarrely put it.

He had stayed on this earth.

The doctor entered the room. This guy was different to Eddie's previous doctor; this one was younger, and far better-looking. Eddie estimated he was in his early thirties, and was warmed by his friendly demeanour.

"Hey Eddie, how you doing?"

"I'm alive."

The doctor smiled and stood beside his bed.

"That you are. Listen, we need to talk about what's going on. Did you want to talk... alone?" He nodded to indicate Jenny.

"She's fine here. Just tell me what's up."

The doctor took a deep inhale of breath and let it out slowly. He took a moment to gather himself, his positive façade dropping and fading into a far darker, unhappy state.

"This isn't going to be easy news to hear, Eddie."

"Okay..."

"It appears that your body is failing. We have carried out numerous tests and... your liver isn't functioning. Your lungs aren't holding oxygen properly. Your heart isn't pumping blood around your body with enough pace, and the blood itself is lacking enzymes. You have potentially cancerous lumps growing all over your body, on almost everywhere they could grow."

Eddie's eyes narrowed and he glanced at Jenny. Jenny looked stumped, gaping wide-eyed at the doctor, her hands covering her mouth. Eddie knew her well enough to know this was her trying to keep it together. This was her trying to be strong for Eddie.

"Eddie, you are dying, and, whilst there are some experimental drugs we can try, it is unlikely to do anything. Your body is functioning the same way as a sick ninety-year-old. It is simply not strong enough to withstand what it needs to do to survive."

"Why?"

"We don't know, Eddie, we don't normally see this in a man in his early 20s. There is little we can do."

Eddie didn't quite comprehend it. He knew what was going on, but it wasn't completely sinking in. He just stared to his feet, his mind attempting to make sense of it all, firing the doctor's words around in his head.

"Liver isn't functioning," … "same as a ninety-year-old," … "not strong enough to survive," … "cancerous lumps."

"So what does this mean?" he asked. "How long have I got?"

"In my estimation, Eddie, if your body continues to deteriorate at the rate it is, I'd say around two months."

And in that moment his world froze. Everything he had done and lost: his sister, his imprisoned father, his selfish existence. Everything he had not yet done: fall in love, get married, have kids, beat his alcoholism, stop letting Jenny down. Everything ran through his mind, darting in various directions, filling it with chaos.

He couldn't hear Jenny saying his name through his tears. It became an inaudible mess in the background that turned into white noise. He felt like he was floating out of his body, away from the scene, into a world of denial, bargaining, and acceptance.

And, as Eddie looked to his reflection in the window, he could swear he saw the woman looking back.

CHAPTER TWENTY-SIX

*E*ddie lay in the sofa bed, watching an unattractive Jerry Springer guest shout at another unattractive guest. He was bored. He wanted to be out and about and doing stuff. He was sick of being pushed around in a wheelchair and he was sick of being too weak to even stay awake for a trip into town.

The alarm on his watch beeped, indicating that it was 3.00 p.m. He dragged his hand to the basket of medication, fumbling to find the correct drugs for the correct time. Eventually he found them and, without bothering to read their ridiculously long names, he stuffed two of them into his mouth and swallowed them down with water.

Jenny walked in and handed him a cup of herbal tea. He couldn't stand it, but he had heard that herbal tea was supposed to make people feel better. If anything, it just made him resent people who made herbal tea.

"You know, you really should take our bed and let us sleep on the couch. I know we'd be fine here. You really should–"

"It's your house. I'm already enough of a burden on you. I'm fine on the sofa bed. Besides," he continued before she could interject with protest, "I've become quite accustomed to it."

She smiled sympathetically and sat on the arm of the sofa bed, peering at the television and rubbing his shoulders. The caption read *I blame you for making me cheat with your dad.*

"Why on earth do you watch this?"

"Makes me feel so much better about my life," he joked. "I mean, sure I may be dying, jobless, moneyless, girlfriendless... but at least I didn't sleep with anyone's dad."

Jenny looked at him unsurely, not knowing whether to laugh at his attempt at humour or cry at the morbid nature of his thoughts. She had always been able to look at him and just know how he was feeling, but for the first time, he didn't seem himself. His eyes didn't look at her like his eyes did, and his smile didn't feel like his smile.

"I'm going to go make some pancakes, you want some?"

"Go to hell you fucking bitch."

She froze halfway through the doorway. Had she just heard him right? She stared at him, completely confused.

He looked back at her helplessly.

"I'm so sorry," he pleaded, a look of complete shock taking over him. "I don't know why I said that, that wasn't me, I-"

"Maybe it's the drugs."

"Maybe..." he said, then became angry. Who was she to say anything about his treatment? Who was she to say anything about what he was doing? Who was she, a homosexual living with another woman, to cast any kind of opinion on anyone else?

"I doubt it, you ugly dyke."

Jenny's jaw dropped; her mouth was agape. Had he just called her a dyke? She couldn't understand it; Eddie was the person who had supported her the most when she came out and announced that she would be living with Lacy. He was the one who stood up to other people for her. And here he was, calling her a dyke?

"What's gotten into you?"

Eddie rose to his feet. Jenny pressed herself away from him against the wall; he literally rose from vertical to horizontal without any help from his arms. He strode toward her with sudden, unexpected energy, shaking his head.

"Why would I support a filthy little faggot like you?"

Before Jenny could muster any more shock or disgust, before she could even convey how hurt and offended she was, she was struck in the face by a photo frame that had previously been on the fireplace.

She looked to the fireplace, which was across the room from Eddie. There was no way he could have thrown that.

"Eddie?" she whimpered. All in a sudden moment, she felt unsafe, like she never had before.

"Eddie's not here right now."

The ornaments around the room: chairs, tables, photo frames, the television, the locks in the windows — all of it shook.

Jenny pressed herself against the wall, slid to the floor, tears streaming down her cheeks. Her arms shook, fear consuming her, dread taking control.

"Eddie?"

"I don't know what's happening..." he cried. "Please help me, Jenny, please help me..."

Before Eddie could say another word, he rose into the air. His head was forced backwards and his neck bent at discomforting, unnatural, obtuse angles. In an abrupt, unexpected movement, he was flung across the room and into the wall, falling on his back.

"Please... Make it stop..."

Jenny crawled over to him. She took his hand in hers and kissed it.

"Eddie, it's okay," she said. "I'm here, it's okay."

With that, the shaking stopped. The room became still until there was nothing but the sound of Eddie sobbing with Jenny.

Had she seen what she had seen? The whole room shaking, a photograph flying on its own, and Eddie levitating, without any control, flung across the room, knocking into the wall?

She didn't believe in the paranormal. She didn't believe in what you couldn't see — but she had seen it. She had watched it with her own eyes. This wasn't some kind of shared hallucination; Eddie was in trouble.

"Eddie…" she said, stroking back his hair and dabbing gently at a cut that had begun to bleed on his forehead.

"Jenny?" he replied just as helplessly, his eyes groggy.

"I think we need to call back those paranormal friends of yours," she said with a mixture of fear and reluctance. "I think we need help."

CHAPTER TWENTY-SEVEN

*E*ddie sat at the table with a steaming cup of coffee, holding a blanket around himself. Even though the heating was cranked up and everyone else was having to remove their jackets, he was freezing, shaking, out of both coldness and fear. He couldn't see himself in the mirror because every time he looked, he saw her.

Not that he wanted to see his reflection. He knew he looked awful by how everyone stared at him.

He was pale. The bags under his eyes were grey. His skin clung to his bones like it was stretched around them. He looked and felt terrible. This thing had sucked every bit of energy out of him.

Derek and Levi sat across the table, leant forward, concerned, watching Eddie, who was sat between Lacy and Jenny, both of their arms rubbing his back. Derek was wearing his smart attire; waistcoat, tie, top button done up. Levi was next to him in t-shirt and jeans, playing with what looked like a microphone connected to a tape recorder.

"We appreciate you calling us." Derek said, as professionally as he could. "I understand why you rejected our ideas, and I'm sorry if we didn't come across as you would have liked."

"It's our fault," Eddie managed, his nose blocked and his voice coming out faintly. "We are the ones who didn't listen."

"Before we resume, I need to ask you some questions to see how far along we are in the process. Eddie, have you looked in the mirror today, or yesterday, or–"

"She's there." Eddie knew what Derek was getting at before he needed to finish the question. "Every time I look in the mirror I don't see me, I see her."

Derek bowed his head. His face tightened, as did his fists, and his leg began wobbling. He kept shaking his head, going to speak then not.

"I fear it may be too late," Derek reluctantly announced.

"What?"

"The entity is no longer fighting for your place on this earth — it has taken your place and it is waiting for you to die. Eddie, this entity is now inside you. You are sharing your body with it."

Eddie was weak, fragile, and helpless, and this only made him feel worse. He was speechless,. How could he be sharing his body with something else?

"Have you said anything nasty? Anything that you perhaps didn't know you were saying?"

"Yes," Jenny answered for him, still wounded from the words that he had unknowingly said to her.

"Okay." Derek looked to the floor then back to Eddie. "This is going to be tough and it may not work. You need to understand, Eddie, that you may not survive this, not in your state, not when it's this late in the game…"

"What are you suggesting?"

"An exorcism. We are going to have to perform an exorcism on you."

Eddie looked to Jenny, then to Lacy, hoping for some help

or indication as to how he should react. They both looked back at him with equally empty faces.

"Like I said before, we have no promises Balam will lose his interest in you. This will not get your sister back. Maybe in the future, but... right now, our priority is getting this thing out of you. And it may already be too late."

Eddie hesitated.

"Fine. When?"

"We have no time to lose. We will set up now, then we will start during the night. At 3:00 a.m."

"Why 3:00 a.m.?"

"Because that is the witching hour. That is when this demon will be at its most present. As will your gift."

"My gift?"

"You are paranormally vulnerable, Eddie. I stand by what I said. You perhaps don't realise it now, but you could potentially have the ability to take on hell itself."

MILLENNIUM NIGHT

CHAPTER TWENTY-EIGHT

*E*ddie looks at his watch.

2.59 a.m.

It is now the year 2000, but he has had no time to celebrate. He has been going all night and he is getting tired — yet he is so close. This is the point of the night he has been waiting for. This is the witching hour.

The first thing Derek taught him about mastering his abilities was the advantage he had between the hours of 3:00 a.m. and 4:00 a.m. It is the time the demons came out to play, yes; but it is also the time at which his powers would match theirs.

And he feels it.

As soon as 3:00 a.m. comes, it's like a surge of electricity soaring through his body. It's like his vision has an additional layer of infrared over it, like he is the master of all that is malevolent and wicked in this world.

He lifts out his cross and stands over the demon, who lies on the floor in the girl's body. He puts a leg either side of the girl's torso and directs the cross at it.

"Enough!" he declares. "Enough, you piece of hell-tainted shit. Leave this girl alone!"

The demon roars at him, a roar with multiple voices that makes the room shake.

This time Eddie is not afraid. He knows what he needs to do. He is going to defeat this demon. He is going to free this girl and liberate his sister's soul after all this time.

This demon is strong, but so is he.

Cassy, hold on. I'm coming.

"Adeline, this is it." He looks into the beast's eyes. "This is the final push. This is when I need you the most. We are going to fight it."

His watch beeps, announcing the arrival of 3:00 a.m. He closes his eyes and takes a deep breath in, his blood heaving like fire through an empty building, consuming everything in its path.

"Help me, God, for I am your servant. Please free this child from this filthy creature."

"Who you calling filthy?"

The demon rises and pushes Eddie onto his back. Eddie does not stay down for long. He regains his composure and resumes his strong posture, holding his cross out.

"You, you filthy coward!" he says, his voice filling the room. "Free this girl, you ugly bastard! Free this girl you disgusting, vile, filth-ridden whore!"

The demon levitates Adeline's body off the ground and floats toward Eddie. It looks directly into his eyes, no more than inches from his face. They look at each other like two boxers before a fight, like two lions fighting over territory, two equal armies charging against each other with nuclear power at their fingertips.

They look at each other like this is the end.

"Free this girl. In the name of God, I command you, free this girl!"

"Give it a rest."

"Free this girl! In the name of God!"

"Kiss my filthy cunt you son of a whore!"

He takes a big, deep breath and projects his words into the face of Balam and the face of all that he stands against. He projects his resentment into the face of evil. In the name of God. In the name of Adeline.

In the name of Cassy.

"Free her! Free her! In the name of God, free her!"

With a humungous growl, the room rumbles. The mouth of the girl widens and a grey cloud flies out. The girl's body drops to the floor and the scars instantly fade.

But it is not over.

The grey cloud surrounds Eddie, encircles him, entwines him in its rotation, lifting him off the ground.

"Take me!" Eddie sends his voice out into the whirlwind of the room, objects clattering back and forth, a tornado of destruction in the demon's wake.

And with that, the grey cloud forces itself into Eddie. It enters through his nose, through his mouth, through his ears; everywhere it is able.

On the floor beneath him, Adeline awakens. She lifts her head and looks around. Fear grips her. She is tangled in the hurricane of anarchy, trapped with despair inside the circulating objects.

She looks up at the man held off the ground before her. She looks to the man called Eddie, the man she knows has saved her. She looks to him with admiration at first, then terror as she recognises it is him no longer.

His eyes burst red. His fingernails turn into claws and his teeth grow sharp. He comes down to the ground with a shuddering halt.

"Silly girl," say the words of Balam through the body of Eddie. "Silly, silly girl. Now I get to look you in the eyes as I kill you."

Eddie's voice becomes deeper and obscured. He is no longer

there. Balam has found a new host — and a stronger, more powerful one at that.

1995

CHAPTER TWENTY-NINE

*E*ddie, Jenny, and Lacy watched on in awe as Derek and Levi set up the living room. Tape recorders were stationed around the room, restraints placed in the corners of the sofa bed and crosses placed on the wall.

As Levi set up a video camera, Derek approached Eddie.

"What's all this for?" Jenny enquired.

"The tape recorders are to catch EVP, standing for electronic voice phenomena," Derek replied. "The restraints are to keep Eddie in place when the demon surfaces, and the camera — well, the camera is partly to capture our findings for the university. But it is also to protect us in a court of law should anything fatal happen."

"Anything fatal?" Eddie's eyes widened.

"Yes. In case you die. Shall we begin?"

Derek indicated the sofa bed in the centre of the room.

Eddie took a few small steps, cautiously surveying the gear they had set up. His hands fiddled with each other and his head twitched. He could feel his arms shaking with nerves.

"Come on in, Eddie," Derek encouraged.

Eddie felt Jenny's hand on his back. He closed his eyes and took a deep breath, stepping slowly toward the bed, sitting on its edge.

"Lay down for me," Levi requested. Eddie slowly did as he was asked.

Levi fastened Eddie's wrists to the corner of the sofa bed, tightening them. He made his way to Eddie's ankles and secured them with the same strength.

Eddie felt more vulnerable than he had throughout the entirety of this process. He lay there, unable to move if he wanted to, staring at the ceiling. A mouthful of sick came to his mouth and he swallowed it back down. He could feel the belt, tight around his wrists, the buckles clattering with the shaking of his arms.

He wanted to be somewhere else. Anywhere else.

"I would like you to stand behind me," Derek told Jenny and Lacy. They obliged.

Derek stood over Eddie, rolled up his sleeves, and produced a book.

"Most glorious prince of the heavenly armies," Derek whispered faintly, closing his eyes and lifting his head upward toward the heavens. "Saint Michael the Archangel, defend us in our battle against principalities and powers, against the rulers of the world of darkness, against the spirits of wickedness in the high places."

He placed his hand softly on his forehead, his chest, then his shoulders, creating the cross upon his body. Eddie weakly gazed up at him.

"Ladies, I have a request," Derek said without taking his eyes away from Eddie's. "You do not speak or move unless on my instruction. You do not talk to it, you do not listen to it, and you do not interact with it. Do you understand?"

Jenny and Lacy nodded.

"Please, it is imperative you indicate that you understand."

"We understand," they both said.

"Now to the demon that dwells within." Derek clutched a cross in one hand and his book in the other. "I speak directly to you."

Eddie gawked up at him. He felt nothing. No change. No presence he had felt previously. Nothing more than his normal weakness. He was numb.

"I don't know what you're expecting, mate," Eddie announced with a peculiarly chirpy voice. "But I don't got a clue what you are on about."

"What is your name?" Derek asked.

"My name is Eddie," he replied. Jenny frowned at the sound of his accent; it didn't sound like Eddie's.

"No, it is not. I command you, tell me, what is your name?"

Eddie chuckled. "Eddie, mate. Eddie."

Eddie's eyes flickered as he felt himself slip away.

"In the name of Jesus Christ, the God and Lord, strengthened by the Immaculate Virgin Mary, I command you, tell me your name."

"Fuck you."

"Mary, Mother of God," Derek was now shouting his instructions. "Of blessed Michael the Archangel, of the blessed apostles Peter and Paul and all the saints – I beseech you, tell me your name!"

Eddie screamed multiple screams from multiple voices, his chest raising and his mouth opening wide.

"With the powerful authority of the ministry, with confidence undertaken in repulsing the attacks and deceits of the devil, God arises and commands you — what is your name?"

Derek took a step forward, reaching out his cross. "In my name, in my Lord's name and in the name of the child of God you have stolen, tell me your filthy name, demon!"

"My name..." Eddie croaked, his head slowly tilting to the side. "... Is Lamashtu. Goddess of death of unborns and newborns, night demon and bringer of disease. And I intend to use my new entity to bring forth death among the endowed!"

"Well, Lamashtu, my name is Derek – and I am here to stop you."

CHAPTER THIRTY

"*L*adies, I need you to repeat the words 'deliver us, oh Lord' after each time I speak, do you understand?"

Jenny and Lacy frantically nodded, clinging onto each other, digging their fingers into each other's back.

Derek gripped his cross, aiming it at Eddie's occupied body.

"Deliver us, oh Lord."

"Deliver us, oh Lord," said Jenny and Lacy in faint echo, their voices shaking.

"I need you to be stronger! Deliver us, oh Lord!"

"Deliver us, oh Lord!"

"Better."

Derek clutched his cross, grasped it, narrowing his eyes and striding forward. Eddie's eyes had fully dilated. His skin had turned grey, his hair black and greasy. Newly formed scars seeped through his arms, dripping blood upon the sheets below him.

"From all sin."

"Deliver us, oh Lord!"

Eddie's voice projected a deep chuckle through the room.

"From all your wrath."

"Deliver us oh Lord!"

Eddie lifted both his arms, snapping out of the restraints, liberating its wrists from its binds. Levi's backed up, leaving Derek as the only one between the demon and the innocent bystanders pressed against the far wall.

"From sudden and unprovided death!"

"Deliver us, oh Lord!"

The restraints around Eddie's ankles flung off and the demon was free. His chest rose up, leaving his head, his arms and his legs dangling beneath him.

"From the snares of the devil, from anger, hatred and all ill will, and from all lewdness!"

"Deliver us, oh Lord!"

Eddie's chest continued to rise until he was levitating half-way between the bed and the ceiling.

Jenny and Lacy's jaws fell, and they wished to be anywhere but in that room at that moment. They feared for their lives and they feared for Eddie's. They did not take their arms away from each other for a moment, trembling together.

The camera Levi used to film short-circuited and flickers of electricity spat at Levi, sending him reeling backwards, clutching his eye.

"From lightning and tempest, from the scourge of earth-quakes, from plague, famine, and from war!"

"Deliver us, oh Lord!"

Derek's mouth turned into a snarl and he thrusted his cross at the demon. The room rattled, photo frames fell over, chairs vibrated across the floor.

"By your birth, by your wondrous ascension, by the coming of the Holy Spirit, the Advocate, on our day of judgement. Deliver us!"

"Deliver us, oh Lord!"

Derek placed his book upon the floor, and nodded at Jenny and Lacy clinging to each other behind him, as if to signal well done. He stepped toward Eddie's ascending body and placed his cross upon it. The sound of burning hissed from Eddie's body as it plummeted back to the bed.

Eddie's face lifted, sneered, then roared at Derek. Derek was taken off of his feet and sent soaring backwards across the room. The objects of the room spun and Derek had to dodge the coffee table.

Every piece of furniture, every object, every scrap, everything in the room, was a hurricane battering furiously between Derek and Eddie.

Derek turned to Jenny and Lacy, their despairing eyes full of terror, and he bowed his head.

"It's no good, it's too late," he spoke solemnly, shaking his head. "It's taken him. Eddie is not here anymore. It's won."

Jenny's eyes filled. She turned her head and buried herself into Lacy's chest, who placed her arms around her and squeezed.

Derek peered at Eddie's body laying still through the chaos of spinning that separated them. If he could not get to it, there was nothing he could do. It was done.

Through a whisper only he could hear, he gave a final prayer.

With a delicacy he had not yet shown, he knelt as close to Eddie's ear as he could without being caught in the debris and whispered softly:

"Eddie, you need to return home."

Eddie did not react.

"Eddie, you need to return home. We will save your sister at another time. For now, return; or you will be trapped forever."

DATE AND TIME NON-EXISTENT

CHAPTER THIRTY-ONE

*E*ddie's eyes opened. Every part of him hurt. He could feel the harsh, bumpy stone leaving imprints and cuts upon his palms. He lifted his head and rubbed his eyes with the back of his hands.

He looked around. He did not know where he was, though it felt familiar to a place he had been twice before. Yet, this time it was different. It was hot. It was fiery. And he felt an overwhelming sense of despair; like all his hope was lost.

He sat upon a large rock. Spewing lava swiped at his feet. All around him were mounds of stone, with various helpless souls laying upon them, crying out for mercy. Above him were large, rocky cliffs, disappearing into the blackened sky. He could not escape the cries. There was nothing but screams of pain — an ambience of agony bombarding his ears, torturing his mind. It was inescapable.

Climbing to his knees, clambering back and forth, he strained to find a way off of the rock. It was no good. Every time he even got close to the edge, lava lashed at his feet.

A few rocks across from him he saw a man in rags, with an overgrown beard, reach out from his rock. The lava spat fire

161

upon his arm. Before the man could even flinch, the lava grabbed his arm like a fist and pulled him under. The man disappeared beneath the liquid magma's surface.

Am I going to be trapped here forever?

Eddie was not sure where he was, but he had a feeling it was somewhere 'beyond.'

Had he died? Not just stuck in a braindead coma floating somewhere between life and death, but actually deceased, damned to a fiery pit for the rest of eternity. Could it be?

Would that mean the woman who had stalked him had won? If he was here, then surely that meant she had his body. She had what she came for.

"Hello?" Eddie shouted out. It was worth a try. The tortured souls did not react — no, they all remained huddled up, screaming in pain.

The lava lashed out at his feet and he instinctively stepped out of its reach. But it was no good. Ash from the lava landed on his ankle and – and, nothing. No pain. No reaction.

How could that be? He had just witnessed a man burnt and pulled into an eternity of agony. How could he…?

That's when he remembered what Derek had said to him.

You perhaps don't realise it now, but you could potentially have the ability to take on hell itself.

He was 'paranormally vulnerable,' or 'paranormally gifted' as they had otherwise stated. What's more, Derek had hypothesised that Eddie could take on Hell itself.

So if this was the underworld, the eternity of pain, then maybe Eddie could fight it.

Maybe he had the ability to be different to the man he saw taken by the fire.

Maybe this was his dominion, and here he was able to be what he never could be on Earth.

He reached out with his hand and held it over the lava. It did not spew at him, it did not grab him, nor did it attempt to burn him. Slowly but surely, he descended his hand until he touched the lava's surface. He closed his eyes, ready for the pain.

Nothing. No burning, no lashing out, not even a tinge of discomfort.

He peered downwards at the lava. He wondered.

If Jesus could walk on water...

He rose to his feet and lifted his first foot out, away from the rock he had awoken upon. He positioned it carefully upon the lava and found that it was able to balance. He placed his next foot down and stood upon it.

This was even better than walking on water; he was practically walking on fire.

He took another step forward, then another, building up tempo, accelerating until he was running at speed. All the people trapped on the rocks reached out to him with their feeble hands and begged. He ignored them, too enchanted by what he was able to do.

His weakness was gone. There were no signs of aching in his legs, shaking in his arms, and no hesitation. He was sprinting over the volcanic lava and nothing could stop him.

He looked upwards at the large, rocky cliff in front of him. He had no idea why or how, but he knew he needed to find a way to the top of it. As if by a miraculous answer, he began to float. He rose upwards and upwards, flying into the musky air and landing upon the cliff that had previously towered over him.

Before him were hundreds of figures, almost identical to the woman that had stalked his consciousness and plagued his coma. Men, women, monsters, creatures. All dark, greasy, and stinking of hatred. Eddie could sense it, the evil. He could feel it surging off of them and hitting him like a bucket of boiling water. They weren't all in human form — many of them had parts of animals, some parts Eddie didn't even recognise.

As Eddie stepped forward, they all flinched. They cowered away from him. A hell full of demons and they were struck with fear by the sight of a simple man.

"Where are you?" he screamed out, hearing his question echo back at him.

Nothing. No demon offered themselves up, no creature stepped forward, no beast dared drop their cowardice.

"I know you are here!" Eddie said. His fists were clenched, resolve strong, and he felt his body filling with power. "Come on out!"

He was almost high on the supremacy he felt rushing through his blood. His body stood tall with authority, and he wondered just how well he could command these monsters.

He held his hand out and the ground shook. The demons separated, and one of them came floating toward him.

It was her.

The long, greasy, black hair, the grey skin, the scars, the wounds, the overwhelming sense of evil — it all indicated he had the correct demon.

He threw his arm downwards and she was flung to her knees, like a dirty beggar praying to its master. It cowered before him, shaking, shivering as if frozen cold.

"You dare to take my place on earth?"

It said nothing. It just trembled, its head rested against the floor, hands over it, not daring to move or go against the command Eddie had over these creatures of hell.

"Now I am going to ask you this one request, and it is your only chance at my mercy."

He held his hand out and scrunched it into a fist. The demon's throat tightened, and it clutched at it as it rose into the air, suffocating.

"Where is Balam? Where is my sister?"

Lamashtu shook its wicked head, a face full of fear and defiance.

"You fear Balam? Well, fear me!" Eddie screamed with all he had, clenching his fist tighter and tighter, forcing Lamashtu's neck to close up.

"You think Balam will hurt you for betraying him? You fool! You will cower before me before you cower again to Balam!"

Without warning, a gust of wind threw itself over him, bringing the whisper of Derek's voice with it.

"Eddie you need to return home," it spoke delicately.

"No!" he bellowed with all his might. "Lamashtu, you will bring forth Balam. *Bring him to me now!*"

Lamashtu shook its head vigorously, its body convulsing under the pull of Eddie's tightly scrunched fist. Eddie could feel his nails digging into his palm, the bones in his fingers shaking under the strain from which he clenched.

"I will not leave here without her!"

Then Derek's voice came again through the wind, floating through him like a ghost through a body.

"Eddie, you need to return home."

"No, I will not leave Cassy here!"

"We will save your sister at another time. For now, return; or you will be trapped forever."

Eddie's gut twisted into knots, his mind torn, his tearful eyes fixated on the suffocating body he held in the air before him.

I love you so much, Cassy.

He knew he needed to leave. Derek was right; he would be trapped forever.

I'm sorry. I'm so, so sorry.

Eddie threw his fist to the side, sending Lamashtu flying over the edge of the rocky cliff and into the spewing lava.

With a disapproving look over the demented fiends backing away from him, he dropped his head and closed his eyes.

CHAPTER THIRTY-TWO

*E*ddie opened and gasped. He sat up, withdrawing a long intake of breath, sucking in every bit of oxygen he was able. The mass of objects swirling around the room dropped to the floor, Derek stood over him clutching a cross, Levi backed up into the corner, and Jenny and Lacy clung to each other against the far wall.

"Guys?" he offered.

"Eddie? Is that you?" Derek held his arm out cautiously.

"Yes. It's me. It's gone. I did it. You were right."

Without a moment of hesitation, Jenny and Lacy ran over and flung their arms around him, hugging him so tightly he could barely breathe.

"Are you okay?" Jenny asked.

"I'd murder a cup of tea."

"I'm on it," Lacy said, and rushed into the kitchen.

Eddie looked over at Derek and Levi. They sat against the wall, willing their heavy breathing to subside. Eddie could tell by looking at them that they had been through an ordeal. They lifted their heads back and closed their eyes, enjoying the success of the moment.

Then Eddie turned to Jenny. She was welling up. She smiled sadly at him, then looked to the ground.

"I thought I'd lost you," she admitted. "Again."

"Hey." Eddie lifted her chin up. "You didn't. We won."

Jenny nodded. She threw her arms around him and held on for dear life. Eddie put his arms around her in return and smiled triumphantly.

Jenny abruptly leant back. "Oh, sorry, am I hurting you? I forgot."

"Jenny, I feel fine. I don't feel weak or anything. You can hug all you want."

With a smile that sent away the tears from her eyes, she flung her arms back around Eddie and held him close for dear life.

"I'm so sorry, Eddie. I'm so sorry."

Eddie said nothing. He just embraced her, enjoying having a friend that cared so much.

MILLENNIUM NIGHT

CHAPTER THIRTY-THREE

*A*deline sits over her saviour and watches him grow lifeless. Balam has taken him; she is saved, but at his expense. She shakes and shakes his body, but he does not move.

Eddie looks down at her. He sees his body lying motionless. He sees her crying over it. He sees her desperately shaking him. He floats over the body, watching her think he is dead.

He is far from it.

To his left he sees his enemy, floating with him. It has three heads: one a bull, one a man, one a ram. The bull aggressively puffs air out of its nostrils. The ram sneers and the man snarls. Together, they growl. Its horns shake and its fists clench, its body scarred with marks of war.

"Balam." Eddie utters. His fists clench and he shakes with power.

"It is you," announces the man head of the demon before Eddie. "Commander of Hell, he who attempts to take his throne."

"And you're a king of Hell, commanding over forty legions of demons, all of which cower before me. I have grown even stronger since I defeated your slave, Lamashtu. Do you dare take me on?"

Balam opens the mouth of each of its heads and roars toward Eddie, sending him floating back against the wall.

He charges back toward Balam, refusing to be forced back.

"Give me my sister!" Eddie commands with all the authority he can force into his voice.

Balam's fists clench and shake, opening, surging red flames toward Eddie. Eddie lifts his hands and the flames half and fall away.

"That the best you got?" Eddie taunts the demon.

Balam growls again, this time not to intimidate, but to show his aggressive displeasure at being well-matched. He throws forward more flames.

Eddie lifts his arm and swipes, causing the flames to cease. He throws his arms forward and Balam thwacks against the far wall, dropping to the floor pathetically.

Balam raises its heads and looks to Eddie.

"Free my sister!"

Eddie raises his arms, forcing Balam into midair, rotating and rotating, faster and faster, till the ram screams, the bull snorts, and the face begs for mercy.

"Free my sister!"

Balam's body turns to a blur, bashing against the wall with each turn, spinning faster and faster.

"I command you, bitch of Hell. Release her!"

Balam screams out, its voice getting caught on the wind of its spin. The room turns into a tornado of chaos, objects turning to weapons against Balam as they get caught in the circle of the whirlwind it creates.

Eddie even chuckles a little as the ram head squeals in agony.

"It is done!" Balam replies, and Eddie drops its body to the floor.

From within it, a body rises. It is translucent, vacantly existential, a bare form of a spirit. But to Eddie, whatever form it is, it is instantly recognisable.

"Eddie..." speaks the voice of his sister, still the age she has been kept at for her eternity of suffering.

Eddie wipes his tears and holds out his hand. Cassy puts hers on his, but her spiritual form falls through it, unable to touch his affection.

"Thank you..." she whispers.

Tears meet his cheeks — the emotion accumulated throughout his childhood, his adolescence, and his adult years turn into one solitary look of love.

With a stare and a smile, Cassy evaporates upwards, transported to the comfort of heaven — or so Eddie hopes.

You're free.

"This is not over," Balam informs him, clambering to its knees. "I will return. I will return with armies and we will take you down."

"I look forward to it," answers Eddie.

Balam drops its heads, goes up in flames, and with that, it is no more. It has disappeared. The room is still. The objects that had spun so ferociously now lay still, and Eddie can now return to his body.

Adeline whimpers and cries over Eddie. Eddie slowly lifts his head.

"Don't cry for me, Adeline," he says.

Adeline's eyes open. She clings to him, hugging him tightly and gratefully, thanking him repeatedly.

"Thank you, thank you, thank you! You saved my life!"

Eddie leans up and props himself against the wall. He runs his hands through his hair and over his face, gathering himself.

"Oh, it was..."

Eddie goes to say 'a piece of cake,' then recalls it wasn't quite that simple.

"It was my pleasure," he says instead.

"Thank you! Thank you so much."

"Oh, stop it." Eddie smiles warmly. "Your mum's downstairs."

Her face lights up and she bursts out of the room. The rumble of quick steps down the stairs is followed by the living room door opening, followed by the loud, happy tears of the girl's rejoicing mother.

He uses the wall to drag himself to his feet. He rests a hand over his back and leans over slightly, rubbing the ache. He looks over the room at the mess, the chaos, the destruction. He would hate to be the one paying that bill.

He heads out of the room and slowly makes his way downstairs. He opens the door to the living room and looks in.

Beatrice clings to her daughter like she is never letting go. Tears protrude from her eyes, and she is so caught up in pleasure at her daughter's safety that she doesn't even notice Eddie peering in.

Eddie decides it's best to leave quietly. Beatrice will want to thank him, and he doesn't do well with gratitude. He slowly opens the front door so as to be as quiet as possible and makes his way out into the morning sun.

A new year, a new millennium. He takes a moment to breathe in the fresh morning air, to smell the rain hitting the ground all around him.

Cassy is free.

He straightens up his tie and takes it one foot at a time.

1996

CHAPTER THIRTY-FOUR

*E*ddie stood over his sister's grave with his hands in the pockets of his trench coat. He hadn't long until Derek needed to take him back to the university for his afternoon classes, but he would never miss his annual visit. This was the first time he had visited her with a clear mind. His hair was neatly parted, his top button done up beneath his tie, and he could still smell his fresh new flat on his clothes.

"I love you, sis," he told the headstone, laying his flowers down and walking away.

In the car park, his red Nissan Micra awaited him in the space where he had left it. He loved his car. It wasn't much, but it was his.

Before he got into his car, he paused. He closed his eyes and took in the moment. He was about to go back to university to complete his demonology degree. After that, he had a very pressing commitment — dinner with his best friend and her girlfriend. It had taken him a long time, but he had finally arrived; he was happy.

"Eddie?" came a voice from behind him. He turned around to see Derek approaching.

"Derek?" he said, confused. "I was just on my way back now."

"I needed to speak to you away from the university. What I'm about to say has not been sanctioned."

Eddie's eyes narrowed. He was confused. What on earth could he need to talk to him about?

As if answering his thoughts, Derek handed Eddie a newspaper, instructing him to turn to page nine. Eddie did so and, at the bottom of the page, he read the headline:

CRAZED MOTHER BECOMES LAUGHING STOCK OF TOWN AS SHE CLAIMS HER DAUGHTER IS POSSESSED.

"Has anyone investigated?" Eddie asked.

"Oh yeah, the church has been, they say she's full of it." Derek leant against the car next to Eddie. "They haven't sanctioned it."

"Well if the Church hasn't sanctioned it-"

"I never told you this, but the Church didn't sanction you, either."

Eddie let this sink in.

"So why are you telling me this?"

Derek looked around, gathering his thoughts. He stroked his neat goatee for a good few seconds before speaking.

"I think it's time we stopped sticking you with books to pass a degree, Eddie."

"What? But I've been working so hard."

"Books are for people who can't do it. We both know that's not you."

"You mean... you want me to come watch this girl's exorcism?"

Derek smirked and chuckled to himself.

"No, Eddie. I want you to *perform* this girl's exorcism."

Eddie's jaw dropped. He froze. Him? Performing an exorcism? He had no field experience, besides the one occasion he was involved and ended up in Hell.

"I don't know…"

"Yes, you do," Derek said assertively. "You have a gift, Eddie. And it is time we started exploring it."

Eddie smiled. Derek was right. He did have a gift. If he could help people, he had an obligation to do so. No, more than an obligation; he had a desire to.

"Where do I start?"

JOIN RICK WOOD'S READER'S GROUP FOR THE FREE AND EXCLUSIVE PREQUEL

Simply visit www.rickwoodwriter.com/sign-up and sign up

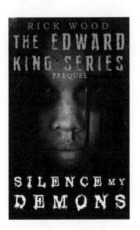

BOOK TWO: DESCENDANT OF HELL
OUT NOW

EDWARD KING

BOOK TWO

DESCENDANT OF
HELL

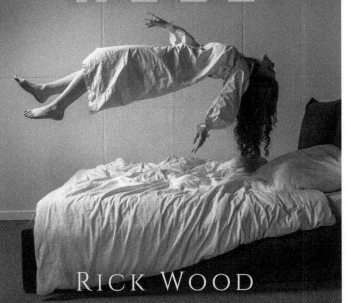

RICK WOOD